BILL DOYLE

⊙RIME THROUGH TIME™

TRAPPED!

THE 2031 JOURNAL OF OTIS FITZMORGAN

LITTLE, BROWN AND COMPANY

New York ⤳ Boston

Text copyright © 2006 by Bill Doyle
Compilation, illustrations, and design copyright © 2006 by Nancy Hall, Inc.
Crime Through Time is a trademark of Nancy Hall, Inc.
Developed by Nancy Hall, Inc.

Little, Brown and Company

Hachette Book Group USA
1271 Avenue of the Americas, New York, NY 10020
Visit our Web site at www.lb-kids.com

First Edition: November 2006

ISBN-10: 0-316-05754-1
ISBN-13: 978-0-316-05754-7

CW

10 9 8 7 6 5 4 3 2 1

Printed in the United States of America

ACKNOWLEDGMENTS

A thank-you of historic proportions to Nancy Hall for making this book and the Crime Through Time series a reality. To Kirsten Hall for her insightful grasp of the overall picture, to Linda Falken for her skillful editing and amazing eagle-eye for detail, and to Atif Toor for bringing the books alive visually.

Special thanks to the editors at Little, Brown: Andrea Spooner, Jennifer Hunt, Phoebe Sorkin, and Rebekah Rush McKay, who are always dead-on, always incisive, and never discouraging. And thanks to Riccardo Salmona for his constant support.

THE SPACE ELEVATOR TERMINAL WAS BUZZING WITH PEOPLE AND HOVER-CARTS.

"Watch out!" a woman screamed.

She leaped to the side as a speeding hover-cart almost ran her down. The driver 'bot didn't even touch the brakes, and the woman shook her fist angrily as it zipped by. No one else but me seemed to have noticed the near-collision. Then, in a second, both the cart and the woman disappeared back into the crowd.

The long hall of the Carl Sagan Elevator Terminal was buzzing with about a hundred passengers. Most were rushing about, worried about catching their Climber on time. Others stared out the floor-to-ceiling windows. They oohed and aahed, mesmerized by the view of Earth thousands of miles below. A few passengers touched the walls and seemed surprised by the rough feel of the knotty wood.

"Why'd they use wood in this space station?" I heard a little girl ask her father.

"This is the new frontier," he told her. "The builders wanted this place to look like the Old West, one of the last frontiers on Earth. That's why they covered the walls with fake wood and that's why..."

They walked down the terminal and out of earshot, but I knew the rest. The Old West theme was why the restroom signs looked like they came straight out of a saloon. Why the chairs that lined the walls were replicas of rockers from the 1800s. And why the hover-carts, which carried luggage and passengers to the gates, didn't beep. Instead, they neighed like horses.

I almost laughed as a human-looking worker 'bot plunked a large object down on the desk where I sat at one end of the hall. Even the 'bot was wearing a cowboy hat on its metal head. When

5

I saw what the 'bot had left behind, I really did laugh. It looked like a weirdly painted giant set of those novelty chattering teeth. Each putrid green tooth was the size of a paperback book.

Carefully, I ran one gloved finger along the top row of teeth. Without warning, the razor-sharp incisors clamped down. I barely had time to yank my hand free.

"Whoa!" I shouted and counted my fingers to make sure they were all there.

"Isn't it beautiful?" I looked up to see a portly passenger standing on the other side of my desk, gazing adoringly at the jaws. He wore a black suit and had a full head of silver hair. Tufts of hair were also sprouting out of his ears—a sure sign he'd taken too many NuHairGro pills.

Beautiful is not the word I'd use, I thought, eyeing the scary piece of art. I was careful to keep my face and hands far away from it.

"Is this your . . . art?" I asked him.

"Yes," he said. "I'm James Bennett."

MR. BENNETT GAZED FONDLY AT HIS ARTWORK.

"I'm sorry. You really can't take this on the Elevator," I said in the friendliest way I could. "The trip down to Earth will take six days. Too many chances for someone to get bitten by this... this..." What the heck was it? The dentures of a monster?

Mr. Bennett sneered. "It's called SHARP TEETH. The artist is that computer H1267 that everyone is talking about. You clearly don't understand that SHARP TEETH represents the human spirit as it faces the challenges of space exploration."

He's right, I thought. My major in college was art, but I didn't get that at all.

"I absolutely refuse to leave it behind," Mr. Bennett said, putting his hands on my desk and leaning toward me. "I just paid a fortune for this piece at the big auction. I don't suppose you'd know anything about that."

Of course I did, I thought. After all, that's the reason I was on this space station. The Out-of-This-World art auction had been held last night at the new hotel. It was part of the celebration that marked the opening of the first Elevator to space—at the top of which we now sat.

Most of the art sold at the auction had been created by computers called "virtual artists." But there were also a few objects made by humans within the past two hundred years. My job was to take a look at each and every piece of art—and use my skills as an art expert to make sure they weren't fakes.

Art fraud has been around forever, but it's really taken off in the past few decades. People are copying all sorts of things—paintings, cars, jewelry, medicine, clothes—you name it. There was even a goofy rumor that a fake Eiffel Tower had been swapped for the real one.

Normally, I'd spend New Year's Eve skiing in New Hampshire with my family or training secretly to perfect my detective skills. But in December, the government had contacted me—as they had a couple times in the past. They said their art expert had been hurt in a reality video-game accident. (I think it was Skate Rat's Revenge.) They knew about my "secret weapon" and told me that I'd be perfect for the job. I had agreed to help—especially after they offered me two extra Elevator tickets for my mom and dad. My parents and I were always together during the holidays, and I didn't want this New Year's Eve to be any different.

But now, as Mr. Bennett glared at me, I was starting to question my decision to make the trip.

"I won't be told what to do by a genetically enhanced child," he snapped.

I took a deep breath. "Sir, it's true I'm fourteen years old, and some people might call me a child if they wanted to be insulting," I said quickly before he could interrupt. "But I'm not genetically enhanced. I don't have time to discuss my DNA with you. I still have one more work of art to inspect. And I have to get this plane loaded onto the Elevator."

I gestured toward the magnificent 1925 biplane with wooden wings that stretched halfway across the hall. The plane had been retrofitted with jet-powered hovercraft capability, but its original, sleek design had been

THE BIPLANE

8

kept intact. After all, it was this design that made it a work of art. A 'bot was carefully hauling it toward the entrance of Climber B, which would carry it back to Earth.

COME HOVER WITH US!

When you're looking for the ultimate in hover engine technology, turn to the Cockerell Corporation! Named after Christopher Cockerell—who tested his designs for the first hovercraft in the 1950s with a hairdryer and two cans—our company has been in the air-propulsion business for two whole years!

Just like the hovercrafts that used to ferry passengers across bodies of water, our vehicle comes equipped with mighty whirling fans. Their spinning creates a cushion of air around the craft, allowing it to move in all directions or simply float. AND our new powerful engines are so small and efficient, they can be adapted to nearly any vehicle. Add them to your plane, your boat, or even your car!

But Mr. Bennett seemed unimpressed by the ancient aircraft. "What's your name?" he demanded. "You're acting a lot like a private detective," he said, spitting the last words out like they were something disgusting. Calling someone "private detective" today was like pointing and screaming, "Witch!" at someone in Salem, Massachusetts, in the 1600s.

Starting in the last century, the powerful Notabe family had launched a campaign to convince Americans that private eyes were a security threat. The Notabes had made a fortune by developing ways to clone humans—and they spent that money freely on their pet cause. It took a few decades to finally get their message across, but private investigation had finally been banned in the United States. Detectives had to either give up being detectives—or work for the government.

"I'm Otis Fitzmorgan," I told him, bracing myself for the reaction I knew was coming.

"Fitzmorgan?" His bushy eyebrows shot up. "As in the Fitzmorgan and Moorie family of private investigators? So I was right—"

"I'm extremely proud of my name," I interrupted, "but right now it's not important. I'm a Deputy Customs Official with the Federal Space Agency. That means I check to make sure that nothing phony or dangerous gets on the Elevator. And this, I'm sorry to say, qualifies as dangerous. I'm not going to allow it on board."

10

Mr. Bennett's reaction caught me by surprise. His mouth opened and closed, but no sound came out. He gazed at the mammoth steel doors behind my desk, which led to the Climber, which moved up and down the Elevator ribbon. The doors were large enough to easily fit the airplane, and they were currently open. A giant clock hung above them. It read:

DEPARTURE FOR EARTH: 13 MIN 12 SEC

Mr. Bennett's face collapsed and tears spurted out of his eyes. "But the Elevator is the only way back down to Earth... and I love this artwork so much!"

"Mr. Bennett!" I said, alarmed.

I knew I shouldn't be swayed by displays of emotion, but I was actually starting to feel sorry for him.

I glanced over at my supervisor, Ms. Jenkins, the customs guard who was clearing passengers at the desk next to mine. I indicated that Mr. Bennett should step closer so that we couldn't be overheard. I said in a gentle tone, "I'll tell you what, Mr. Bennett. Let me remove the power source from this...work of art. That way it won't go snapping anyone's head off. The 'bots will load it into the storage area on Level 5. That level isn't accessible from the main part of the Elevator. It will be safe there."

This seemed to soothe him. "Thank you," he said, wiping away his tears. Then I noticed his thin lips forming a small smile. He quickly covered it with his hand. For a second, I wondered if he'd been acting. But before I could say anything, he was gone, rushing over to Ms. Jenkins's security checkpoint, where the other passengers were waiting to be cleared.

MR. BENNETT
SMILED SLYLY.

11

I should've known better, I thought. I can sometimes judge a work of art better than I can judge a person.

Sighing, I called over a 'bot and asked him to put his two-ton arm on top of SHARP TEETH to keep the jaws from opening. I took a screwdriver from my belt and carefully removed the panel at the bottom of the teeth. As I began disconnecting the wires from the battery, I felt a message come up through the floor and into my feet:

CLIMBER B DEPARTS FOR EARTH IN TEN MINUTES. ALL
TICKETED PASSENGERS MUST BE ON BOARD AT THAT TIME.

I ignored this announcement as best I could, which wasn't easy since it was a "smart" message. Only passengers with Climber B tickets like mine could receive it. The words traveled through the floor as vibrations, up the correct passengers' legs and into their heads. There, the vibrations became sounds. It was a great way to keep noise down in the Terminal, but annoying if you were trying to concentrate.

Two minutes later, I'd disconnected the last wire inside SHARP TEETH. I tossed the battery in the trash and removed my micro-probe from a loop in my belt. It was about the size of a cereal spoon, and I placed the thicker end lightly on the artwork. The probe made a gentle chime that let me know the procedure had been successful. I had just given my DNA stamp of approval to SHARP TEETH. I signaled for a 'bot to load it onto the Climber.

Once it was gone, I turned my attention to the last item waiting for inspection. I had been saving this one as a special treat for myself. I threw back the tarp.

Underneath was a larger-than-life marble statue that captured a moment just after the assassination of President Lincoln in 1865. Lincoln himself isn't part of it. Instead, it shows Mary Todd Lincoln reaching out toward John Wilkes Booth, who is leaping backward as if to avoid her touch.

ESCAPE BY A HAIR

Now, this was my kind of art! It was sculpted in 1866 by the famous artist Maginold Moylan. The lines were smooth and elegant, and it actually made you feel something—besides queasy, like SHARP TEETH did. You could really see the anger and confusion on Mrs. Lincoln's face as she grabbed at Booth and just missed him.

It's easy to see why the statue's name is ESCAPE BY A HAIR.

Part of my job was to fill out a Condition Report for the valuable artworks. Filling in the blanks about the statue helped me to determine if the piece was a fake or not.

As the sculpture was loaded onto the Elevator, I thought it was strange that "human hair" was listed as one of the materials. Must have belonged to the artist, I decided.

ALL TICKETED PASSENGERS MUST BE ON BOARD AT THIS TIME.

Done just in time, I thought, as I received another Climber B ticket announcement. I glanced again at the clock above the huge steel doors. It read:

Condition Report

OBJECT ID, IN CASE IT IS STOLEN:

_____

TYPE OF OBJECT: Statue

MATERIALS: Marble; human hair; tin

TECHNIQUE: Carved by artist with chisel and hammer

MEASUREMENTS: base, 10 feet by 8 feet; height, 12 feet; weight, 510 pounds

TITLE: ESCAPE BY A HAIR

SUBJECT: Mary Todd Lincoln and John Wilkes Booth in a box at Ford's Theater

DATE OR TIME PERIOD: 1866

ARTIST: Maginold Moylan

13

DEPARTURE: 2 MIN 35 SEC

I snapped off my plastic gloves. It was time for me to join my parents on board. I could see Ms. Jenkins was wrapping things up and packing up her gear.

"Wait!" a female voice cried. "Come on, Dad!"

A teenager with curly blonde hair, and a short, plump man were rushing toward Ms. Jenkins.

"Now, now, let's not panic, dear," the man told his daughter. As he followed her, he read from a pamphlet about the Elevator. "Did you know the Elevator is more than 60,000 miles high? That's like going from New York to Los Angeles and back—ten times. No wonder the trip takes six days!"

Without a word, Ms. Jenkins cleared the girl and her father through customs.

But when they passed within a few feet of me, I jerked around. I raised my hand urgently to get Ms. Jenkins's attention. Her head snapped up, and I signaled for her to stop them. Something definitely wasn't right.

14

"Halt!" Ms. Jenkins bellowed. She placed a hand on the shock stick slung through a loop in her belt. The man noticed this and started to squeak in terror.

The girl stepped in front of him protectively.

There was no reason to threaten such force. I didn't want things to get violent. I rushed over to them. "Hold on!" I called to Ms. Jenkins.

"Let me handle this," Ms. Jenkins told me and grabbed my arm to pull

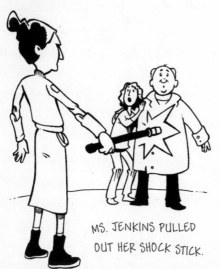

MS. JENKINS PULLED
OUT HER SHOCK STICK.

me back from the man and girl. As she did, I caught a whiff of Ms. Jenkins's petunia-scented perfume.

Her grip was strong, and I spun around. My journal—this journal—flew from my pocket and landed on the floor with a thud! And the mini DogBot I use as a lock flicked off.

About the size of a large box of matches, the 'bot instantly leaped to life. DogBots were the most popular holiday gift a few

TEDDY

years back, and it had been almost impossible to find one. Then it seemed like they were everywhere, and suddenly, people didn't want them anymore. Not me. I had given mine as much artificial intelligence as his little circuits could hold. He was a kind of

pet and went everywhere with me. His brown bio-real eyes—which looked like a baby seal's—clicked open.

"Teddy, stop it!" I commanded. But Teddy was cranky at being so rudely awakened and wasn't listening to me. He bounced about like a flea on his little steel legs.

"Nice toy," the girl said sarcastically, eyeing Teddy. "I think I had one of those when I was four."

But she was nervous. I could tell by the way she was flipping through the pages of my journal without looking down at what she was doing. I wanted desperately to snatch the journal out of her hands, but I was worried that I would just draw more attention to it.

15

TEDDY ATTACKED MS. JENKINS'S SHOE!

Meanwhile, Teddy was facing off with Ms. Jenkins's shoes. They were the new kind that had high heels in the front. It made my shins hurt just looking at them, but I guess some people will do anything for fashion.

"Do you mind?" Ms. Jenkins asked me.

Blushing slightly, I scooped up Teddy, who clicked and squirmed in my hands, trying to break free so he could resume his attack on her shoes. I tucked him back into my jacket pocket.

"Passports, please," Ms. Jenkins said to the man and the girl. With retina scans and other biometrics, there was really no reason for old-fashioned passports. But passengers felt better about having them. "And what was the purpose of your visit?" Ms. Jenkins asked them as she inspected their documents.

The girl gave the man a nudge. "I write travel guides. I'm Robert Noonan, and this is my daughter, Charlotte."

"Uh-huh. Why are you so nervous, sir?"

"This has been our first trip into space," his daughter Charlotte broke in. "I think it's natural to be a little shaky, don't you?"

Ms. Jenkins nodded and removed her security wand from her belt loop. She waved it over them and gave me a look that said, Why did you waste my time? Her search had come up empty.

Just as I knew it would. Her wand wasn't programmed to pick up what I had detected. Embarrassed, I mumbled something to her.

"I can't understand you," Ms. Jenkins said.

16

I took a breath and said loudly, "Mr. Noonan has a piece of fruit!"

Everyone looked from me to Mr. Noonan. Realization dawned on his face. He reached into his coat pocket and removed a kiwi. The guard took it from him.

"Dad!" the girl cried, and then in almost the same breath, asked me, "How did you ever know that was there?"

But even Ms. Jenkins didn't know about my "secret weapon." So I kept my mouth shut.

"Are you aware that it is illegal to transport foods grown on the Elevator Terminal back to Earth?" Ms. Jenkins asked coolly.

Charlotte's face went red. "How would we know that? This is the first time we're taking the Elevator down to Earth!" While her dad

CHARLOTTE AND MR. NOONAN

cowered behind her, Charlotte continued, "Where is that law about food written down? Is it on the wall?" She pointed to the blank wall. "No! Is it on our ticket?" She waved the ticket in our faces. "No! Is it in this journal?" She flipped through my journal and scanned a page. "No—"

She broke off, and her eyes widened slightly in surprise. She looked up at me and opened her mouth as if to speak. I knew she must have spotted something on the page about my training to be a private detective.

Questions whirled through my mind. Was she going to reveal my training to Ms. Jenkins? Would she use the information against me to get herself out of trouble?

And then Charlotte closed the journal and shoved it into my hands. Without a word, she looked at me. She raised one eyebrow, as if to say, The ball's in your court.

Meanwhile, Mr. Noonan was nervously clutching his daughter. His beady eyes shot from Ms. Jenkins back to me. "Are you going to arrest us?"

"No, of course not," Ms. Jenkins said. "Just please be more careful next time you travel with us. And thank you for using the Space Elevator."

I think I was more relieved than Charlotte and her father. Mr. Noonan threw one end of his scarf over his shoulder dramatically. "Come along, Charlotte," he said. "We have a Climber to catch!"

I watched the two of them heading into the Elevator. The same one I would be boarding in a moment.

This is going to be a long ride, I thought.

19

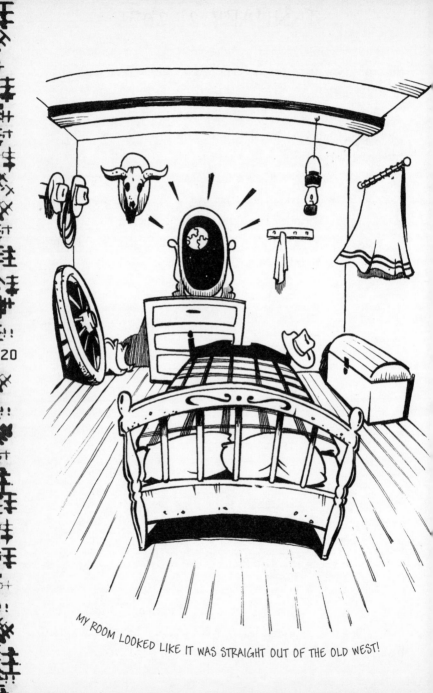

MY ROOM LOOKED LIKE IT WAS STRAIGHT OUT OF THE OLD WEST!

Teddy woke me up this morning by

yanking on my ear with his rubbery mouth.

"Enough!" I told him, but he knew better. He continued to bounce around my pillow like a metal flea that's had too much coffee. I'm not a morning person, so I've programmed Teddy not to stop bugging me until I'm up and moving.

"Okay, okay," I said. "Good boy." I sat up in bed and rubbed my eyes. Satisfied that he had done his job, Teddy turned in my lap and lay down.

"Lights up slowly, please," I said to the computer, and the lamps around the room began to glow and grow in strength.

My room on the Elevator was pretty big—plenty of space to fit a bed, a desk, and a dresser. I even had my own bathroom. Fake wood was used for everything, just like in the Terminal. So it looked like a small hotel room—in the Old West.

But the real attraction was the window. A small mirror had been placed on the outside near the top. It was angled to give passengers a view of Earth without their having to get out of bed. And the view was spectacular.

We were orbiting Earth. But because we were tied to the planet's surface by the long ribbon, our position didn't change. I could see the western half of the United States and part of Asia.

With its swirling cloud patterns, gorgeous blue oceans, and rich green and brown continents, the planet was beautiful. It floated in black space like a welcoming light at the end of a tunnel. But I didn't have that happy feeling of returning home that I had expected I would.

Why should I be excited about going back to a place that wanted to destroy my dreams?

Ever since I could remember, private investigation had been outlawed. And lately there had been a growing movement to deal much more harshly with those who broke the law. Soon I wouldn't be able to risk even my simple training exercises—like helping one of my teachers track down her stolen painting. I just couldn't put my family in that kind of danger.

Yesterday's brush with discovery had made me realize that even more. If Charlotte tells anyone what she read in my journal, I'll be finished. But my family has been keeping journals for generations, and I don't want to be the first one to stop.

Not for the first time, I wondered what Judge Pinkerton would make of this whole mess. Of course, I'd never met her. The famous federal judge and creator of the Private Detective Academy had lived to be over a hundred years old, but she'd died before I was even born. Still, I felt like I knew her. She was a presence in all of my family's journals.

FIRST PRIVATE EYE ALSO A SPY!

Born in Glasgow, Scotland, Allan Pinkerton came to the United States in 1842 and settled in Chicago, Illinois. Pinkerton was an abolitionist, and his place of business also served as a station for escaping slaves on the Underground Railroad. Pinkerton (left) founded the first private detective agency in 1850. Ten years later, he foiled a plot to assassinate his friend and president-elect, Abraham Lincoln (right). After the Civil War began, President Lincoln hired Pinkerton to form a secret service to spy on the South.

JUDGE WAS A PINKERTON!

And I've become kind of the keeper or librarian of all these journals. The actual journals themselves are safely hidden back in our home in New Hampshire. But I've downloaded all their content, including the sketches and attached items, into my personal hard drive, which I keep in a pendant shaped like a shark tooth that I wear around my neck. To keep my hard drive from being broken into,

I've never connected it to the Net. And even though I down-load my old journals onto my hard drive, I use old-fashioned paper and pen instead of a handheld computer to keep the current one. Like my hard drive, this means my journal isn't connected to the Net—so no one can hack into it.

MY HARD DRIVE

23

After a few more minutes of sitting there, my grumbling stomach finally finished what Teddy had started. It got me completely out of bed. I went to the small closet and pulled out my dark green intelli-cloth shirt, plaid jacket, and brown pants. It wasn't the most stylish outfit in the world, but at least it wasn't the FSA uniform I'd had to wear in the Terminal. Plus the clothing had self-cleaned the night before and had that fresh, piney smell I liked.

I held out my journal, and Teddy clamped his jaws around the side that opened. He would keep his mouth closed around the book, keeping it locked and safe from prying eyes.

"Okay?" I asked him. He blinked twice, the signal for yes. I tucked Teddy and my journal into my jacket pocket and walked to the door.

I said, "D'en," and the door slid open. Most computers were smart enough to recognize this contraction for "Door open." It was kind of lazy to say, "D'en," but you can only say, "Door open," so many times a day. And the Elevator's computer was supposedly one of the fastest and smartest ever created. It had to be. It ran our communications, heating, water, food, air—all the systems we needed to survive up here, thousands of miles above Earth.

I knew there were twenty-nine other passengers on board Climber B, so I was surprised to find that the hallway leading from my room to the interior elevator was empty. I guessed people were either still sleeping or down in the common areas. The elevator door opened with a DING! and I went in and pressed the button for Level 3.

Climber B is actually like a five-story box-shaped building that travels up and down a ribbon made of a lightweight material called "carbon nanotubes," which is a hundred times stronger than steel. Right then, I was leaving Level 4—the sleeping quarters. I had no choice but to go down. You couldn't get up to Level 5 from inside the Elevator. Besides holding crates, boxes, and bags, it's where a lot of the Elevator's equipment is located.

On Level 3, the elevator door slid open onto a small hallway that led around the corner to the gym. In front of me was the Common Room. An Elevator worker had pulled out a partition, cutting the room in half. One side was for quieter activities—like reading or chatting—and the other had louder entertainment options—like semi-real video games.

I glanced into the quiet section. It looked like a small restaurant that had been combined with someone's modern living room. There were several tables where many adults were eating, watching news

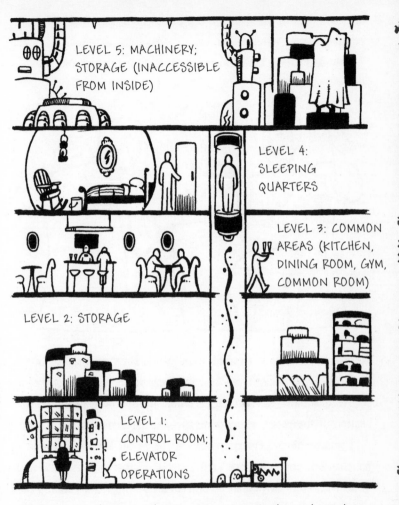

LEVEL 5: MACHINERY; STORAGE (INACCESSIBLE FROM INSIDE)

LEVEL 4: SLEEPING QUARTERS

LEVEL 3: COMMON AREAS (KITCHEN, DINING ROOM, GYM, COMMON ROOM)

LEVEL 2: STORAGE

LEVEL 1: CONTROL ROOM; ELEVATOR OPERATIONS

projections, or chatting with Interactive News Anchors about the latest events. I saw Mr. Bennett viewing a holo-exhibit of modern art. Other people lounged on couches scattered around the room, gazing out the observation window that took up most of one wall. Two adults were on a surround-show platform and acting in a virtual soap opera. Holo-actors whirled around the two of them as

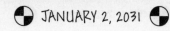
they took part in the drama. Across the room, I spotted my mom and dad talking with another couple over cups of coffee.

My dad raised his hand in greeting, and my mom mouthed, "How'd you sleep?"

I gave her the best smile I could this early in the day. She smiled back, knowing it was best to let me wake up at my own speed.

With another wave to my parents, I headed over to the other section of the room, where a mostly younger crowd had gathered. And where things were not nearly as peaceful. There were four couches but only one large central table on that side. A semi-real video game unit (a real game unit would be too dangerous up here) had been installed in one corner. A holo-gunslinger was there, shouting out taunts like, "Which of yer yeller-bellied so-and-sos thinks yer can outdraw me?"

But none of the five people in the room seemed interested in challenging the gunslinger. Everyone was too busy with a real-life drama.

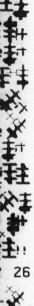

"I want my chair back!" a boy with spiky black hair and a squat, muscular build was shouting.

The target of his anger was none other than Mr. Noonan. He was perched in a master control chair at the head of the table. The chair allowed the person to control the lights, temperature, sound effects—everything

A BOY WAS SHOUTING AT MR. NOONAN AND THE HOLO-NURSE.

27

about the room. But Mr. Noonan didn't seem to care about all the buttons—he looked too terrified to move. His hands clutched the armrests and his knuckles were as white as his face.

The nurse hologram was standing next to him. "What seems to be the problem?" she asked in a soothing voice. "Please select from the following. One: upset stomach. Two: headache. Three—"

The boy interrupted, the veins in his neck popping out. "You can talk to the nurse on the other side, where all the other adults are!"

Before I could say anything, a girl with long jet-black hair stepped forward. "Maybe you should just leave him alone?" She spoke timidly, making the suggestion as if it were a question.

"And who are you?" the boy fired back at her, pointing a finger in her face. The girl looked stunned by his rudeness. When she didn't answer, the boy shouted into the air, "Computer, who is this girl?"

The pleasant voice of the computer answered,

LYSA A. BENATO. AGE FOURTEEN. SHE IS THE DAUGHTER OF MAXINE—

"Computer, stop!" Lysa commanded, her voice rising. She looked even more flustered when the computer continued speaking.

—BENATO, VICE PRESIDENT OF SALES AT URBANE COSMETICS.

"I gave the computer an order," Lysa said, bewildered.

Looking smug, the boy gazed at her and folded his arms across his chest. It was clear from his bulging biceps that he had taken one too many muscle-enhancing pills. Which could also explain his aggressive behavior. "My family owns the hotel at the top," he said, "so I'll decide what happens. My commands override all others."

Now I knew who the kid was: Yves Jackson. He was my age, but he acted like he owned the place. Well, in a way, he does—or at least, his family does. The Jacksons put up tens of billions of dollars to complete the Space Elevator. In fact, so much of their money

28

LYSA AND YVES FACED OFF

A TALL, SKINNY BOY TOLD THE HOLO-NURSE TO SHUT OFF.

had gone into the project, they'd been given sole own-ership of the hotel at the top.

"I need some medicine!" Mr. Noonan suddenly bellowed.

The holographic nurse looked at him. "This does not appear to be a medical emergency," she said.

I stepped toward them, about to say something, when I was stopped by another new voice. "Nurse, please turn off." It was a tall, skinny boy with limbs that reminded me of a grasshopper's. He had a long face with widely spaced eyes.

The holo-nurse smiled, said, "Have a healthy day," and flickered off.

"Why didn't I think of that?" Yves Jackson said, then turned to Mr. Noonan and demanded, "Now can you get up?"

"What are you doing? I need the nurse," Mr. Noonan whined at the new boy, who held out his hands in a calming gesture.

"You have to get up!" Yves snapped.

Enough is enough, I thought. "Yves Jackson?" I asked in my most official-sounding tone.

"What?" he demanded.

"I'm Otis Fitzmorgan, an official with FSA. I noticed someone suspicious lurking outside your quarters on Level 4," I lied. A little fib seemed worth it to help out Mr. Noonan.

"And what did you do about it?" Yves said angrily.

"Nothing," I answered with an exaggerated shrug. "I'm no longer on duty."

"Typical!" Yves cried. But my plan worked. Forgetting about Mr. Noonan, Yves threw up his hands and stormed out of the room to check on his quarters.

With Yves gone, the tension in the room instantly came down a couple of notches. And everyone seemed to sigh in relief.

CROCKETT TRIED TO CALM MR. NOONAN DOWN.

The skinny boy gave me a nod of thanks and then turned back to Mr. Noonan. He crouched down next to the man. "Hi, my name's Crockett Vinton," the kid said in soothing tones. "I came up with my folks. They decided to stay behind for a few more days, but I have to get back to the books. I'm in medical school."

"You're a doctor?" Mr. Noonan asked.

"Almost," Crockett answered. It wasn't strange for kids our age to be doctors and lawyers anymore. Genetic enhancements had made some kids more mature. My own genes were straight from my parents—and hadn't been altered. Instead, my mom and dad had been feeding my love of art and detective work since I was a toddler. All the art history books, home training, and museum trips had paid off. They helped me rise to the top of my class and stand out as a government investigator.

"From what I can tell, you're just anxious," Crockett was saying to Mr. Noonan. "You need to relax."

"How can I? This is terrifying! I'm a writer, not an astronaut! Going up, I slept most of the way. But now we're going down! I feel like we could crash at any minute!"

"Are you traveling with anyone?" Crockett asked.

"His daughter, Charlotte, is on board," I answered for the man. "I'd get her but I don't think she's too crazy about me."

Crockett cocked an eyebrow at this but stayed focused on Mr. Noonan. "I'm going to go get your daughter," Crockett told him. "I'll be right back." And he rushed out of the room.

But it didn't look as though Mr. Noonan would be able to wait. I had to do something. I took Crockett's spot, crouching down next to the man. "Hi," I said. "Remember me?"

He nodded but looked too panicked to speak. To make things worse, Teddy chose that moment to pop his head out of my jacket pocket. He greeted Mr. Noonan with a little yap.

"Get that thing away from me!" he shrieked, startling Teddy and sending him skittering to the floor.

"Teddy, go see her." I pointed to Lysa, who was sitting curled up on a couch. "Do you mind watching him for a second?"

TEDDY YAPPING AT MR. NOONAN

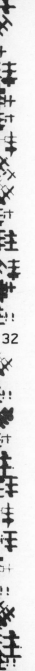

Lysa shook her head and gave me a little smile. Teddy clicked and hopped over to her.

I put my hand on Mr. Noonan's shoulder. "You're a writer, so you must have heard the phrase 'a little knowledge is a dangerous thing,' right?"

"I think a little ribbon is even more dangerous. And that's what this Climber is hanging from! A teeny-tiny ribbon!"

Good, I thought, at least he's able to make a joke. I had an uncle who was afraid to fly. When he found out that it was safer than driving a car, he changed his mind. "How would you like some background on the Elevator?" I asked him. "It might make you feel better."

Mr. Noonan nodded. "Okay, fine. Anything to take my mind off where we are!"

I quickly searched my memory for facts. "To build this Elevator, a spacecraft was launched into geosynchronous orbit over Earth. That's 22,300 miles over the equator."

"You're losing me!" Mr. Noonan cried.

He was right. I was being too technical. I had to keep things simple and positive. "The spacecraft lowered a ribbon made of superstrong material down to Earth as it kept moving outward into space. When the ribbon reached Earth's surface, it was attached to a base station in the middle of the ocean near the equator. Because hurricanes don't pass over the equator, it reduced the number of violent storms—"

"Hurricanes?" Mr. Noonan squealed.

Darn! I thought. I could tell he had been starting to relax. And then I had to go and talk about hurricanes!

I smiled and switched gears. "Two hundred and fifty small mechanical climbers stitched on additional ribbons to widen and

THE SPACE ELEVATOR ON THE RIBBON TO EARTH

strengthen the original one. That took three years. The ribbon we're riding on—"

"The ribbon that's holding us up is thinner than paper, right?" Mr. Noonan asked, but the panic was gone from his eyes, and he seemed more interested than worried.

"That's true, and it's only about three feet wide. But it's

33

strong enough to support a Climber carrying about 30 tons of supplies and equipment."

"And people?" he said, and I could see he was making another little joke.

"Yes," I nodded, chuckling. "And people."

I kept talking about the technical aspects of the Elevator. Slowly he relaxed, and at last, the color returned to his face. He put a now-steady hand on my shoulder. "Thank you," he said as he started to get up. "I do feel much—"

"Get away from him!" Charlotte stormed in, followed by Crockett. "What are you doing to my dad?" she demanded as she strode over to us.

"Otis was calming him down until you came bursting in here like a bully," Lysa said.

"And he was doing a very good job of it," Mr. Noonan added. "I think I'm ready to join the other adults now."

Charlotte looked confused. "Dad..." She reached out to him.

"I'm fine, dear," he said, taking her hand and patting it. "Why don't you just stay here and make friends?"

With that, he walked out and left Charlotte standing in the middle of the room. She appeared embarrassed.

Crockett glanced away. Lysa gave her a long look. Gazing at Charlotte and Lysa, I noticed how much alike they looked. They could have been sisters—twins even—except for their hair color and style of clothing. Where Lysa had straight, jet-black hair almost to her waist, Charlotte had a mass of curly shoulder-length blonde hair.

And now she was on the verge of blushing under those curls.

"Okay," she said to me. "Maybe you made me think something different was going on."

"Is that an apology?" Lysa asked.

Charlotte shrugged defiantly then cracked a smile. "My dad did say I should make friends. Guess I'm not following orders, as usual," she said, her smile becoming a grin.

Her change of mood seemed to take the last of the tension out of the air.

Crockett, Lysa, Charlotte, and I chatted for a while. It turned out Crockett and Lysa are both from New York City and Charlotte is from Seattle, Washington. When the conversation started to lag, a flash suddenly erupted at our feet.

Startled, I looked down to see Teddy winking up at me mischievously. Teddy was equipped with a digital camera and had just snapped our photo.

34

I was about to apologize for Teddy's behavior when Charlotte struck a pose like a fashion model. Lysa gave him a few silly poses, and Teddy's metal tail whacked back and forth in glee. Soon, Teddy was bouncing around us and snapping photos like a full-blown paparazzo.

LYSA AND CHARLOTTE POSING FOR TEDDY

At one point, Charlotte leaned over and said in a soft voice, "Don't think this gets you off the hook for nearly having us arrested for carrying a piece of fruit. I still can't figure out how you knew my dad had that kiwi."

I shrugged. "Lucky guess," I said, not completely truthfully. "What can I do to make it up to you?"

"I'd like to see the art collection," she said as if she were asking for a glass of water. "I want to see the art that was sold at the auction."

The words, "No can do," were on my lips. After all, the artworks from the auction were on two different levels, one inaccessible and the other strictly off-limits to the passengers.

But instead I said, "Sure. Why not?"

36

LEVEL 2 WAS DARK EXCEPT FOR THE SECURITY LIGHTS.

Charlotte's eyes went wide, and she

whispered, "Oh..."

I held my finger up to my lips. "We have to keep quiet. We're not supposed to be here."

We'd just exited the elevator onto Level 2. Only people with security clearance could get here. I'd had to press my thumbprint against the elevator's control pad to gain access to the level, which was like a warehouse. The dull hum and clank of the powerful magnets that controlled our descent toward Earth echoed through the huge room. A 'bot or two whizzed around, but otherwise, we were alone.

"It's awfully dark," Charlotte said, peering into the gloom.

There were no windows, only the large door through which the 'bots had loaded the art sold at the auction. Not wanting to attract attention, I left the main overhead lights off. We'd have to do with the security lights that cast pools of illumination over each work of art. Most of the artworks had been packed carefully into crates and stored on Level 5. But I'd asked the worker 'bots to put the larger objects—like the plane and the statue—on Level 2. Even though I was off duty, I wanted to be able to keep an eye on them.

"Come on," I told Charlotte, and led her over to the biplane. Flecks of the original green paint still clung here and there to the body of the plane, which was shaped like a sleek bird of prey. Charlotte's reaction was what I had expected. "Incredible!" she exclaimed. "This is really fantastic! And you get to be around artwork like this all the time?"

"When I take a job like this, I do," I replied, putting one hand carefully on the wing of the plane. "Honestly, though, I'm not always surrounded by master works of art. I go to classes, like other art students, and go hiking and camping with my friends." I didn't add that I also spend a lot of time organizing my family's detective journals.

"So ...," Charlotte said, her gaze still drinking in the aircraft. "Tell me how you work, Otis."

I guess that's when I started to show off. "Better yet, I'll show you," I said, taking out the pocket watch that my dad had given me on my fourteenth birthday.

"Nice watch," Charlotte said, glancing at me.

"Thanks. It's been passed down through our family for generations." I detached the microprobe from my belt loop. I placed the thick end of the probe against the watch and proclaimed, "Watch this!"

There was a soft chime from my probe. "There!" I announced. "See this screen?" I asked, pointing at the color readout. "It tells me that this watch is made of steel, glass, a little crystal, and small amounts of white paint."

I could tell from Charlotte's face that she wasn't impressed. Desperate to entertain her, I kept talking. "The probe uses a laser.

• ART FRAUD NEWSLETTER •

Fakebuster Tools

In 1998, an Egyptian papyrus was brought to London for auction. Spectroscopy provided by a Raman microprobe revealed that the blue and green ink used on it wasn't available until 1936, meaning ancient Egyptians couldn't have made it. Other tools used to detect art fraud include:

Provenance research

Stylistic analyses

X-rays

Ultraviolet fluorescence

Infrared micro-spectroscopy

Microanalysis—analysis of pigments and binding material (both inorganic and organic)

Fiber identification

It shines on a sample area, and the scattered radiation, or photons, are analyzed. This tells me what materials were used to make the object. Also, I can check out pigments or dyes. Were they around when the piece of art was created? None of the tools I use will harm the object itself, which is important."

Stifling a yawn, Charlotte turned back to the plane. "Can I touch it?" She was already moving her hand toward the tail.

I should let her, I thought. That'd put a stop to her boredom. But I said, "I wouldn't recommend it."

Her hand was still moving. "Why not? You did."

"There's a field set up around each item. And it will deliver a jolt of electricity that will knock you off your feet."

She lowered her hand. "Well, I guess that's a good reason."

"The field has been programmed to allow only people with the correct DNA through," I said.

"We use DNA in another way, too," I continued. "After I've inspected a work of art and determined it's real, I put an invisible stamp on it. The stamp is

DNA TODAY HOLO-ZINE

DNA Isn't Just for Eye Color!

In each of the trillions of cells in your body is a blueprint that makes you who you are. It's called DNA. There are billions of different DNA combinations that decide things like hair and eye color. Everyone—except identical twins and clones—has his or her own DNA combination, and that's what makes you unique.

DNA is superstrong because it's copied over and over as cells multiply. This stability makes DNA perfect for nonbiological uses—such as a stamp that works like a one-of-a-kind signature. That's right! You can now sign important documents with your DNA. Better than fingerprints, which can smudge, DNA is also harder to copy and will be an amazing weapon in the fight against fraud.

39

microscopic, and it contains my DNA. It's like adding my signature to the piece. I can use my microprobe to check that my DNA signature is in place at any time."

I ran the probe over the plane. Another pleasant chime let me know my DNA stamp was still there. "Everything's fine," I told her. Once again, I was showing off, but I couldn't seem to help myself.

"What would happen if your probe told you one of these pieces of art was a fake?"

"Whoever found the real artwork would get a huge reward from the insurance company—and I'd be out of a job."

"But working for the government isn't the job you want anyway, is it?"

"What makes you say that?"

"Just something I read somewhere…" Her voice trailed off, but her eyes locked onto mine with a challenging look.

I knew, of course, she was talking about what she'd seen in my journal when she was flipping through it at the security clearance area. But before I could say anything, she walked away.

I followed her over to the ESCAPE BY A HAIR statue.

"Now, this is something," she said.

"What's it make you feel?"

Her eyes glinted, but she just shrugged. She started walking to the next object, which was a carved totem. As she moved away, the air stirred around the statue. I caught a whiff of the light smell of the soap she used.

CHARLOTTE SEEMED IMPRESSED BY THE STATUE.

40

"I think you'll—" I froze in my tracks. "It can't be..."

Charlotte turned to look at me. "What's wrong?"

I ran my microprobe over the statue and confirmed that my DNA stamp was in place, but I knew I was right. My limbs felt heavy, and my head swam. I pointed with a shaking finger at ESCAPE BY A HAIR and managed to say, "This statue is a fake."

"Are you serious?" she asked. "How do you know?"

I sniffed around the statue.

"What are you doing?" she asked, as I smelled the air again.

"Forgers have been able to copy all kinds of materials. They can get past most physical inspections. But there's one thing they haven't been able to copy, and that's the smell of certain materials."

"I don't follow you."

"I have a secret weapon I use in my job. So far, the FSA has managed to keep criminals from finding out about it."

"What's your secret weapon?"

"My nose."

"Your what?" She asked, looking doubtful.

"My nose!" I almost shouted. "I can pick up and identify smells as well as any bloodhound."

"You're kidding—" She broke off as understanding flashed in her eyes. "So that's how you knew my dad was carrying food in his pocket!"

I nodded.

INK STINK

Different inks and materials have different odors. Just a sample of the smells I try to detect when inspecting art for fraud:

MARBLE (STONE): Has a clean, sharp odor—like an ice cube from a freezer packed with steaks.

MAHOGANY (DARK WOOD): Smells like a handful of rich, compacted earth.

VARNISH: A light acrid odor if the artwork is more than 100 years old. A stronger smell that fills my nose indicates a newer work.

GREEN INK: Reminds me of sweat or a gym locker.

BLUE INK: Makes me think of our musty old boathouse in New Hampshire.

YELLOW INK: Gives off a sugary smell, almost like candy.

When the materials above are listed as part of the art but the odor isn't there—my nose tells me something's fishy!

41

I removed a small blade from my belt. In one fluid motion, I hacked off a small piece of the statue.

"You can't do that!" Charlotte gasped.

"I'm confirming what my nose tells me to be true."

I walked over to the minilab in the wall, hoping that it would be stocked with the materials I needed. I found a petri dish and dropped the hunk of statue into it. I could use my microprobe as a heating device. Now I just needed a food source.

"Do you have any kind of food in your bag?"

"All I've got is sugar," Charlotte replied, handing me a packet from her bag. "It's rare to find real sugar these days, so I always carry some around with me to put in my tea."

I tore open the packet and dumped it into the petri dish. I adjusted my probe and aimed it toward the dish.

BLAM!

There was flash of light, and the piece of statue seemed to explode.

I ZAPPED THE SHARD WITH MY PROBE.

Shocked, Charlotte jumped back.

"Sorry," I told her. "I meant to say, watch out."

In less than a second, the bit of statue had been reduced to a grayish brown pile of what looked like sand.

She gasped. "What just happened?"

After slipping on a plastic glove from the minilab, I ran my

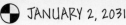
hand over the sculpture. "This statue is definitely a fake. Someone used biological nano-material to recreate a near-exact copy of the original."

Charlotte shook her head. "Can you say that again for the back of the class?"

I took a deep breath and tried to explain it more clearly. "Nano-material is made up of smart cells that are manmade. They're alive, but they've been constructed by scientists."

"Like mini living robots?"

"That's right. Nanobots are extremely small. If you lined up thousands of them end to end, they might only be the width of a human hair. They may be small, but because they're living, they need to eat. Nanobots can't resist a food source. It overrides whatever their secondary programming might be. It's kind of like a survival instinct. If you introduce a liquid food source, they act like a swirling school of starving sharks."

"I remember now. We studied this stuff in grade school," she said. "Wouldn't a group of nanobots this big be worth more than the statue itself?"

"Yes," I said. "And no one has ever been able to copy a DNA stamp before. These nanobots must be the most advanced kind."

I was shaking my head and staring down at the petri dish. I could be in serious trouble. "Come on," I ordered. "I have to tell my parents."

We rushed back to the elevator. As the doors closed, I jabbed the button for Level 3.

I didn't speak on the way up. Charlotte nudged me with her elbow. I looked at her, and she gave me a small, reassuring smile. "It's going to be okay."

43

I wished I could be so sure.

With a DING, the door slid open.

"There you are!" Yves cried, putting one meaty hand on my chest. "You lied to me! You sent me up to my room for no—"

YVES THE BULLY

I knocked his hand away. "Yves, I don't have time for this," I said through clenched teeth.

His face went red and he took a step closer to me. "You'll make time—"

This was ridiculous. We pushed past him and walked into the Common Room. The partition had been removed, and the two rooms had been turned into a single large one. My parents were at one of the tables chatting with Charlotte's dad, who appeared to be feeling much better. I could see Lysa curled up on a couch and Crockett standing in the corner talking with the holo-nurse.

As I tried to figure out how to tell my parents about the fake statue, the elevator dinged, and I heard Yves say, "What are you doing here?"

Many of the adults had looked up as we came in. My mom and dad were looking at me expectantly with half-smiles. Then they must have noticed the alarm on my face. They both stood.

"Honey, what is it?" my mom asked.

I opened my mouth to speak—and saw the most terrifying thing in my life.

Without warning, the bodies of each and every adult went rigid. Their arms were straight at their sides, as if they were being jolted by an electrical shock.

Then in flash, they all collapsed.

It was like a watching a forest of trees fall under the invisible axe of a ghost. If they were standing, like my parents, their bodies simply crumpled to the floor. If they were seated, they either pitched forward or slumped back in their chairs. It was over in about one second. Only five people remained standing—Crockett, Lysa, Charlotte, Yves, and I.

SUDDENLY ALL THE ADULTS COLLAPSED!

"Mom! Dad!" I shouted and rushed to my parents.

Lysa screamed and ran to her mom. Mrs. Benato had been seated at the table eating something and had fallen headfirst into her plate.

"Dad!" Charlotte yelled as she raced over to Mr. Noonan.

"Nurse!" Crockett shouted above the din. But the holo-nurse had disappeared.

Only Yves looked rooted to the ground. "I didn't say you could do this!" Clearly in shock, he was shouting at the adults. "Get up at once!"

Crockett pushed him aside and walked over to Mr. and Mrs. Jackson. They'd been in the middle of a virtual TV show, but the holo-figures had dematerialized, and Yves's parents were in a heap on the floor.

"Nurse!" Crockett called again, but the hologram of the nurse didn't reappear. "Computer! Emergency!" Again, no response.

"What's happened to them, Crockett?" I asked from across the room. My voice sounded panicked and scared.

Flustered, Crockett shook his head. "I don't know." He straightened the limbs of Mr. and Mrs. Jackson and made them as comfortable as possible. Then he walked over to me.

"The Jacksons seem to be breathing fine," he told me. "It's as if they've just gone to sleep."

I had just placed pillows from the couch under my parents' heads and was crouching by my mom. Crockett knelt next to me.

"Let me examine your mom," he said. I nodded, and he placed a hand on her wrist and took her pulse. "It's fast but steady and strong. Now for her eyes..."

Crockett gently pulled back my mom's eyelids to examine her pupils—

And what I saw made me gasp. My mom's eyes were almost completely black.

46

"Whoa...," Crockett breathed.

There was a cry of shock from behind me. It was Yves. He must have been looking over my shoulder. Now, he stumbled backward and hit his head against the wall. He slid to the floor, muttering something that I couldn't understand.

I glanced back down at my poor mom. But this time, I didn't panic.

On second look, I could see it was just my mom's contact lenses that had gone black, not her eyes.

WHEN YVES SAW MY MOM'S EYES, HE STUMBLED BACK IN SHOCK.

Following a hunch, I ran the end of my probe over the back of her neck. There was no interference. I gently lifted my dad's head and ran the probe over the skin of his neck. Once again, the screen showed no interference.

"I'm not picking up any signs of their 'quists," I told Crockett.

He shook his head. "That's impossible. Even when you turn off a 'quist, it will still register on probes."

All the adults I knew had a 'quist implanted at the base of their skull so they could connect to the Internet. They wear special contact lenses to see "screens" and can send e-mail, visit Web sites, write documents—everything they used to do with a keyboard and a mouse—just by moving their hands, lips, and eyes.

That's why the device is called a 'quist—which is short for ventriloquist. People look like bad ventriloquists when they communicate with the computers, because their lips are moving. But you can't hear what they're saying.

And now something had gone wrong with my parents' 'quists. "Help me get their contacts out," I told Crockett.

After we removed the contacts, I was relieved to see that my parents' eyes looked perfectly normal.

We moved around, checking on the other adults. Lysa was crying silently over her mother, and Charlotte was on a couch, her dad's head cradled in her lap. All the adults had the same symptoms—including blackened contacts. We plucked them all out and tried to make everyone as comfortable as we could.

"What is happening?" Charlotte asked, looking down at her dad's face.

"I think the 'quists have made all the adults sick somehow," I said from between my parents.

"Why weren't the five of us affected?" Yves asked. He was still sitting against the wall.

"Because you have to be eighteen to get a 'quist implant, genius," Charlotte shot back. But she seemed to realize she was being too harsh, and her voice softened. "We're okay because we're not old enough to get a 'quist, and the 'quist is what made the adults collapse."

Lysa looked at me miserably. "What do we do?"

"I think—," I started to say.

Yves lumbered to his feet. "I'm in charge here!"

Charlotte rolled her eyes and ignored Yves. "Keep talking, Otis. What do you think we should do?"

All eyes were now on me.

"First things first," I said. "We have to check out the Controller," I said.

"Who?" Lysa squeaked.

"The Controller is the operator down on Level 1," I replied. "He's the one in charge of driving the Climber. We have to make sure he's okay."

I walked to the intercom on the wall. You actually had to press a button and speak into the box. I tried contacting the Controller, but there was no response.

I turned back to the others. "Let's go down to Level 1 and check on him."

Everyone—even Yves—nodded.

Crockett looked up from putting a cushion under Mr. Bennett's head and said, "You four go ahead. I'll stay here with the adults and try to figure out what's wrong with them. Good luck."

I hated to leave my mom and dad, but we couldn't sit in the

CROCKETT VOLUNTEERED TO STAY WITH THE ADULTS.

49

Common Room and do nothing. Once the four of us were on the elevator, I pressed my thumb on the pad next to the button for Level 1.

"What are you doing?" Lysa asked.

"Level 1 is a restricted floor. You need security clearance to access it."

The elevator door opened, and we stepped into a short hallway. This floor was meant for Elevator personnel only, so the designers hadn't bothered with the Old West theme. The walls were a stark white that was almost blinding under the harsh overhead lights.

Most of Level 1 was occupied by the computer equipment that kept the Climber moving safely up and down the ribbon.

At one end of the hallway, a sign on a door read: CLIMBER CONTROL.

"The Controller's in there," I said. We made our way to the door and knocked. There was no answer, so I said, "Door open." The door didn't move. I tried pressing my thumb on the pad next to it. Once again, no luck. The door wouldn't budge.

"We're going to have to force it open," I said.

"That's impossible," Charlotte said. "We're not strong enough."

"Let me," Yves said, and stepped in front of us. "I don't go to the gym for nothing." He put both hands on the door and pulled to the side as hard as he could. As I watched the veins in his neck and arms pop, I thought Charlotte was right. You couldn't open a door just by pulling on it.

YVES USED BRUTE STRENGTH TO OPEN THE CONTROL ROOM DOOR.

And then Yves grunted and pulled even harder. Amazingly, the door started to slide open. He was able to move it just enough for us to squeeze through into the Control Room. Charlotte didn't hesitate. She turned her body sideways and slid into the room.

"Good job, Yves," I said. But before he could respond, there was a frightened gasp from Charlotte.

I squeezed through into a small room filled with monitors and blinking buttons, and saw what had startled her. The Controller, a bald man who looked to be about thirty, was passed out in his chair. His body had slipped to one side, and if he hadn't been strapped in, he might have fallen completely out of his seat.

THE CONTROLLER WAS UNCONSCIOUS, TOO!

We straightened him out and checked his condition. He was breathing fine, but just like the adults up on Level 3, his contacts had gone black. I removed them and turned to the mammoth control panel that took up the wall in front of the Controller's chair.

51

My eyes ran over the sleek operating system, taking it all in. I tried pressing a few buttons and touching different screens. Nothing happened.

"Someone has destroyed the communications system and put the Elevator on autopilot," I said. "There's no way to stop the Elevator, and there's no way to talk to anyone on the outside."

"But what about oxygen or heat? Are those systems working?" Lysa asked.

"Yes, thankfully, those are all intact. We have plenty of oxygen for the trip down," I assured them. "And the artificial gravity is working just fine."

"Why do I know you're about to say, 'But...,'" Charlotte asked.

"Because I haven't told you the worst yet," I answered. "Whoever destroyed the communications system had to do it in person. That means the bad guy has to be somewhere on board the Climber."

Lysa gasped and covered her mouth with her hands.

"Let's head back to the Common Room," I said. The thought that there might be a criminal wandering around the Climber made me even more worried for my parents.

"I think I'll stay here," Yves announced. He plopped down in the extra seat next to the emergency airlock that led outside.

I shook my head. "No, we all need to stick together. Let's go. You can help me carry the Controller up to Level 3 so Crockett can take a look at him."

Grudgingly, Yves stood up. I took the Controller's legs and Yves took his shoulders. In the Common Room, we found Crockett holding a magnifying lens with a mini video screen over a small blood sample.

He looked up as we came in. "Who is he and what's his condition?" he asked.

As we made the Controller comfortable on an extra couch, we told Crockett what we'd found on Level 1.

He gave a grim smile. "My discovery isn't much more hopeful than yours, I'm afraid. I've never seen a bug like this. It's like everyone with a 'quist has been infected with a computer virus."

"But how can that be?" Charlotte asked. "Computer viruses make machines sick, not people."

Crockett shrugged. "In this case, it looks like everyone with a 'quist was redirected to a server. That server instructed the brain to release a chemical dihydrocarbon-6."

Lysa said, "And that's bad because…?"

"The chemical caused a sleeping virus to wake up."

"What are you talking about?" I asked. "What sleeping virus?"

"It must be something we all breathed in on the Space Station or when we boarded the Climber. I checked while you were on Level 1, and I have it. And I'm sure you all do, too."

"Then are we going to get sick?" Yves asked.

Crockett shook his head. "Not as long as our brains don't release that exact amount of dihydrocarbon-6. And, don't worry. The odds of that happening naturally are about six billion to one."

"Can't you just turn the virus back off again?"

"I wish I could, Otis. It's started to multiply."

Charlotte was looking down at her father, who lay on the couch. "Why did the contacts turn black?"

53

CROCKETT FIGURED OUT WHY THE CONTACTS TURNED BLACK.

54

"A 'quist is programmed to shut off if something is harming the user, but for some reason, these 'quists couldn't shut off. I think the contacts were trying to destroy themselves. That would cut off connection to the 'quists and they wouldn't be able to cause any more harm."

"Are the adults' brains okay?"

"Yes, Charlotte. It's just like they've got a really bad infection. I can't tell you everything about it. There's some kind of command attached to the virus's DNA that I can't understand. But I haven't told you the worst part yet..."

"You mean it gets worse?" Lysa asked.

"Oh, yeah," Crockett said. "Much worse. Right now, the bug is happy to live in their bodies. But in a few days, it will move to their lungs and leave their bodies as they exhale."

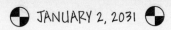

"What are you saying?" Yves asked.

Crockett looked him in the eye. "It's only a matter of time before the virus becomes airborne and kills us all. And when we get to the bottom of the Elevator and they open the doors..."

His voice trailed off, so I finished his sentence for him. "The virus will rush outside, and everyone on Earth will be infected."

55

TEDDY KEEPING WATCH OVER MOM AND DAD

56

This morning, the five of us sat

around the breakfast table in the Common Room. Well, the other four sat. It was hard for me to keep my butt in a chair and not pace when talking about such a huge problem. I think better on my feet.

The Elevator was traveling thousands of miles a day as it continued its journey to Earth. But, on board, we were making zero progress.

The night before, we had carefully moved all twenty-six adults to their beds. Crockett had found IV bags in the medical supplies and attached a bag to an arm of each adult. The intravenous solution would provide nourishment and keep them from getting dehydrated. Crockett had moved constantly from room to room, checking on the adults and making sure that they were comfortable.

The rest of us had tried to catch a few hours of shut-eye. But, with everything going on, that had been almost impossible. I had dragged a chair between my parents' beds, where they lay sleeping. They were breathing like birds, their chests rising and falling a little too quickly, as if their bodies were trying to expel the virus with each breath.

When I had jerked awake this morning, my first thought had been, "Please let Mom and Dad be better." But I could see there had been no change. They were still unconscious. I put Teddy on the chair where I had slept.

Stay with them, I told him using Teddy-speak, a bunch of hand commands that only Teddy and I recognized. My journal would be safe in my jacket pocket without him guarding it for a while.

Teddy blinked at me twice to signal that he understood. If there were any changes, he would find his way to me in the Common Room.

And that's where we all were now. Lysa's face was puffy as if she'd been crying. Charlotte looked stunned and angry. Yves appeared sullen, like a spoiled child whose birthday party has been ruined by rain. And Crockett had circles under his eyes, already showing the strain of trying to care for all the adults.

It wasn't easy to concentrate. Every time someone opened a package of food, a pop-up ad appeared out of the box. I guess when the bad guy knocked out the communications system on the Climber, he or she had also destroyed the pop-up ad blocker. Now there wasn't anything to keep these annoying advertisements from bursting out of every package and box of soda that was opened.

For the first few minutes, the room had been filled with dancing bears, rockets blasting off, and other holograms that yammered jingles like, "Crispy, crunchy and sweet—a taste even aliens can't beat!" and, "The juice! The juice! The juice is on the

THE POP-UP ADS WENT WILD!

loose!" Finally, the ads stopped, and we could get to work on solving our problems.

Unfortunately, Yves was the first to speak. "What's the point of this meeting?" he demanded as he stretched his bulging muscles. "We'll get help when the Climber reaches Earth. The ground crew will open the hatch—"

"And we'll release the virus on the planet," Charlotte interrupted him.

"We can warn them not to open the hatch until they get the situation under control."

"We might not be able to," I said.

"Why not?" Yves asked.

"We could be...," Crockett started, but before he could say "dead," Lysa let out her familiar gasp. He softened his tone and said, "We could be too sick—or worse—to warn them somehow."

"But we don't have 'quists," Charlotte said.

"It doesn't matter," Crockett told her. "It's like I said before. This bug is going to go airborne in the next few days. And when it does, we won't be able to escape it. We'll be just as sick as the adults are."

Lysa slumped in her chair as if all were hopeless. "So what can we do?"

"We can't give up," I said. "We have to find out where the virus came from and who released it. That person might have the cure. So we have to solve this crime."

"You mean act like private detectives?" Yves scoffed, rolling his eyes.

"I mean act like people who want to survive," I shot back.

"Even if we did want to be detectives," Charlotte said, "we can't use most of our modern devices to solve the crime with the Climber's communications system down."

"It's like we've gone back in time," Lysa said.

"You've got a good point. Maybe it's time for us to start looking to the past," I said and thought, Where was Judge Pinkerton when we needed her?

"What?" Charlotte said.

I hadn't realized that I'd said the last sentence out loud. "I was just thinking about how a family friend would deal with a situation like this."

As they all stared at me, I thought about my family's journals, which were safely stored in my hard drive. I scanned through my memory as though I were flipping through the journals' pages. I thought about how different relatives dealt with solving their cases. Fitz had been a fingerprinting expert—but we had no prints here. Zeke could crack codes like nobody's business—but there were no codes to crack. I thought of G. Codd Fitzmorgan—Aha! That's it!

"Dramatic reenactment," I blurted.

G. CODD FITZMORGAN

"What's dramatic reenactment?" Lysa asked.

"Sounds painful," Charlotte said, trying to make a joke.

"I have a relative who used it to help find a pilot who disappeared in 1925," I explained. "In a dramatic reenactment, you act out the events that lead up to the crime."

"Which crime? The attack on the adults? The sabotage of the Elevator? The switching of the statues?"

"What statues?" asked Lysa.

I filled the others in on what Charlotte and I had discovered on Level 2. "I don't think we should consider the crimes separate events," I added. "I think they're all connected. Like links on a chain."

Crockett nodded. "Okay, what do we do?"

"Let's start with the one link in the chain that we all witnessed: Our parents being knocked out by the virus."

"Why don't we start with the ESCAPE BY A HAIR statue being stolen?" Charlotte asked.

I thought about it for a second. "I am absolutely certain that I inspected the real statue up on the Terminal. And I watched it being put on the Climber, so it must be somewhere on board. That's one of the links, but I think we need to start with the adults getting sick."

"I don't know if I can do that...relive them collapsing like that, I mean," Lysa said quietly, looking down at her hands.

"Even if it might help to save them?" Charlotte asked gently. "If we can find the bad guy, maybe he or she will be able to reverse the effects of the virus or at least have an antidote."

Lysa wiped the tears away from her eyes. "Okay," she said, her voice sounding stronger. "I'll do it."

Before she could change her mind, I started getting everyone into position. "Let's all stand where we were when the adults collapsed. Charlotte, you and I had just left the elevator. Yves, you were out there with us, too, remember?"

61

The three of us went out to the hallway, while Crockett and Lysa stayed in the Common Room.

"We walked off the elevator…and, Yves, you said…"

"Hi, how are you?" Yves said with a little sneer.

"Ah…no," Charlotte responded. "You said something nasty to Otis about sending you up to your room."

"That's right," I said, trying to keep us on track. "Then you wanted to talk to us some more, but we went past you and into the room. Like this." I took Charlotte lightly by the arm, and we walked into the Common Room.

Lysa was seated on the couch. Crockett was standing in the far corner, exactly where he'd been the day before. He said, "Lysa and I were already in here—"

I said, "My parents stood up and then—"

"They all fell down!" Lysa cried and put her hands over her eyes as if she were seeing it happen again.

But Charlotte remained calm. She snapped her fingers as if remembering something. "No," she said. "Before they collapsed, the elevator stopped on this level again. I heard the door open, and Yves said something."

"That's right!" I exclaimed, playing the scene back in my mind. "Yves said, 'What are you doing here?' to someone."

"But who?" Crockett asked. "Nobody came into the room."

62

"And we didn't see anyone in the hallway when we left to go down to Level 1," Charlotte added.

We all looked at each other with the same question on our faces: Then who was Yves talking to? Could this be the break in the case we were looking for? One way to find out, I thought, and turned to ask him. "Yves?"

There was no answer. I imagined he might be pouting because things weren't exactly going his way, and I walked out to the hallway.

It was empty. Yves was gone.

Followed by Lysa and Crockett, Charlotte came out into the hall. "Where's our self-proclaimed leader?"

"I was just wondering the same thing," I said. "It's not safe for anyone to wander off like this."

"Maybe he didn't wander away...," Crockett considered.

"Maybe he ran because he's the one who did all this," Lysa added.

"I don't know about that," I said.

"I agree with Otis," Charlotte said. "Don't get me wrong. I think Yves is a real snake. But to spread this virus? Something like that would take lots of brains."

"I'll find him." I said and walked down the hallway toward the gym.

But I didn't have to go that far. Halfway down the hall, Yves had ducked into a small alcove with a drinking fountain. He stood with his back toward me, looking like a student who'd been told to stand in the corner for being bad.

YVES WAS GESTURING!

63

I heard whispering as I got closer. Had Yves gone a little nutty? Was he talking to himself? Then I noticed that his hands were moving as if he were gesturing to someone.

He turned and I saw that faraway look that new 'quist users have. Yves had a 'quist!

He finally saw me through all the data that must be streaming before his eyes.

"Go away!" he cried.

Suddenly, his eyes started going cloudy. It was the virus!

"Yves! Disconnect!" I shouted.

But he scurried out of the alcove and darted past me down the hall toward the Common Room.

"Yves!" I shouted. "Disconnect! Disconnect now! Every second counts! You could be infecting yourself with the virus!"

But he wasn't listening to me. He just kept running.

YVES TRIED TO ESCAPE BY LEAPING OVER A TABLE!

"He has a 'quist!" I shouted to the others who were still standing near the elevator. They looked up startled as Yves raced into the Common Room, and for a moment, they just stared.

Then everything was a blur of motion. We all rushed into the Common Room after Yves. We had to catch him and get him to disconnect.

But Yves's powerful body had made him as fast and agile as a mountain cat. Muscles popping, he leaped over a table. He wasn't going to be easy to nab.

"Stay away from me!" he shouted.

The four of us formed a semicircle around him and were backing him slowly into a corner.

I caught Crockett's eye and made a small gesture with my hand. He nodded that he understood. To distract Yves, I started talking. "Manet was the greatest of the Impressionists but often used subject matter that would be considered trite and clichéd by today's art critics."

Yves looked at me, confused. "What are you talking—"

Crockett moved quickly and crouched behind him. Lysa— normally so mousy and quiet—must have found some reserve of strength. She darted in from the side and pushed Yves. He stumbled back over Crockett and sprawled on the floor.

I dropped on top of him, trying to be as careful as I could. After all, I didn't want to hurt the guy, I was trying to help him.

I put my knees on either side of Yves's chest to keep him from getting up. By now, Crockett was holding down his struggling legs, and Lysa and Charlotte had each taken one of his flailing arms.

"Take it easy, Yves," I told him. "I just need to get the contacts out." Using my thumb and index finger, I pried open one of his eyes. The contact was just starting to cloud over but had not turned black.

Yves stopped fighting me as I plucked out both contacts, cutting off his connection to the 'quist. I handed the lenses to Crockett. "I'll put these in solution," he said.

When we let go of Yves, he didn't jump up. The energy seemed to have drained out of him. I had to help him up into a sitting position.

"What were you thinking, Yves?" I demanded. "Why were you using a 'quist. You knew that you would be infected!"

"I'm different than you...," he said, his words slurring. "Better than..." Yves slumped back, and I caught him just before his head hit the floor. His eyes were closing.

"Wait!" Charlotte cried. "He has to tell us who he was talking to yesterday just before the adults collapsed!"

She was right. Yves might hold the key to the identity of the bad guy. I gave him a gentle shake. "Yves? You have to stay awake." But there was no response. I sighed and carefully laid his head back down on the floor.

"I don't get it," Charlotte said. "If he had a 'quist, why didn't he get infected when the adults did?"

"He must have had the device turned off so it wouldn't be detected when he passed through customs," I said as I got to my feet. "It's illegal for him to have a 'quist because he isn't eighteen."

"But he's above the law," Charlotte said sarcastically.

Lysa added, "But not above getting sick."

Crockett had put the contacts in a glass of solution and now knelt on the other side of Yves. He checked his pulse and examined his eyes. Yves groaned and then was quiet again.

"How bad off is he, Crockett?" I asked.

Crockett looked up at me. "He didn't have the 'quist on long enough to get a full blast of the virus like the adults did. But he still got enough of it. He might not be as sick as they are now, but he'll catch up."

CROCKETT HANDED ME THE CONTACTS.

This might be my last chance. I had to try and get through to him again before he sank into a deep uncon- scious state. I leaned over him and said loudly, "Yves, who did you see when the elevator stopped right before our parents got sick?"

But he didn't respond. His eyes remained closed.

"We have to make him comfortable," Crockett said. "Otis, help me carry him to his room, and I'll start an IV to keep him hydrated."

After we got Yves settled, the four of us met back in the Common Room. Once again, we sat around a table, considering what our next plan of action should be.

"I guess this rules out Yves as a suspect," I said. "After all, he probably wouldn't give himself a deadly virus just to cover his tracks."

"Now what?" Charlotte asked.

A thought occurred to me. "Let me see the contacts." Crockett handed me the glass. I held one of the contacts up to the light. It was clouded over like a dirty window. "We can use this. It has a microchip in it that will let us plug into his 'quist."

"That's crazy!" Crockett cried. "If you hook up to the Net, you'll get infected!"

"You're right," I agreed. "We can't use it to connect to the Net. We don't know where the program that turns on the virus is lurking."

Lysa threw her hands in the air. "So what's left? Everything's connected to the Net."

"Not everything." I was thinking about my secure hard drive around my neck. Maybe I'd made a mistake. I was looking for a way that my family's journals could help us, but I shouldn't have been looking for a single thing. Instead, I should have been searching for the one thing they all had in common. A plan began to take shape in my head.

I told the others what I was thinking.

"That's about the craziest thing I've ever heard. No one's ever done anything like that," Crockett said, but I could see the excitement in his eyes.

Charlotte just grinned. "I'm in," she said. "Let's do it."

I opened an eye wide and moved the contact closer.

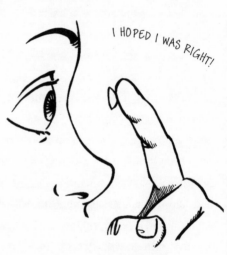

I HOPED I WAS RIGHT!

"No!" Lysa cried.

I stopped. "Lysa, it's okay. Do you want me to go over the plan again?"

"I just don't get it!"

We were all gathered on Level 2 next to the fake statue.

"Okay," I said. "Here's the plan. Since Yves's contact can still be used, I'm going to wear it so I can connect to his 'quist."

"But people use 'quists to connect to the Net, and that's where the virus trigger is!" Lysa paused to bite her thumbnail. "It's too dangerous to go back online."

"You're right," I told her. "But I don't have to. You can also use 'quists to access nearby databases wirelessly."

"But how do you know which one is safe?"

"There is only one computer database that I know I can trust: my own." I knew all the journals my family had kept over the years were secure because my hard drive had never been hooked up to the Net.

"But why do we have to do it in here?" Lysa swept her arms out, indicating the copy of ESCAPE BY A HAIR. I'd turned on the overhead lights, but even they couldn't dispel the gloom. "That statue is so creepy."

"Because I can use the 'quist to reprogram the nano-material from the fake statue."

"To do what?"

"Like I said before, I can reshape it into...into..." It sounded too crazy to say it again, and I couldn't finish my sentence. "You'll just have to trust me on that point," I told her, and put the contact in my eye before I could think about it anymore.

Instantly, a flickering screen popped up. It was like someone had laid a sheet of clear plastic over half my vision. There was a small blinking target symbol.

Charlotte asked, "Are you okay?"

"I think so," I lifted my hand, and the target symbol whizzed away. "Wow. That was fast."

Lysa said, "You must have used Gesture Technology before."

"Sure, but never this close up." The microchip in Yves's contact allowed the use of Gesture Technology in place of a mouse or a keyboard. But normally when you buy a 'quist, there's a two-week training program so you can get used to operating it, kind of like taking driver's ed before you get your license.

I moved my hand more slowly and sent the target symbol over to the file options. A blinking question mark appeared on the screen.

WHO ARE YOU? a small voice asked inside my head. This must be Yves's 'quist device.

I moved my lips silently in response. "Otis."

The tiny voice said, YOU DO NOT HAVE ACCESS PRIVILEGES TO LOCKED FILES, OTIS.

"I don't want access privileges. This is an emergency. I need help."

There was a beep, and then the voice said, EMERGENCY PROTOCOL. ESTABLISHING TEMPORARY NEURAL LINK.

"Wait!"

YES?

"Will this harm the owner of the 'quist?"

70

FSA SERIES 450 TEST
Question 905:
Gesture Technology (GT) turns eye blinks, head movements, finger flicks, or other gestures into computer commands. It's been decades since it replaced the mouse as the way to move things around on a computer screen. But only recently have systems become accurate enough to pick up on 99.9 percent of possible gestures. What group of people prompted such huge strides in development?

A. People with physical challenges that limit their body movements

B. Video gamers who demand instant responses to keep up with the action

C. Office managers and others who need to organize data quickly

B is the answer! Video gaming is one of the most popular forms of entertainment and generates tons of money for new development.

NO. SHALL I CONTINUE?

"Fine."

NOW CONNECTING TO THE NET.

"NO!" I shouted out loud. Beyond the screen, I could see my three friends jump slightly at the sound of my voice.

I focused again as the tiny voice asked, DO YOU WANT TO CONNECT TO THE NET?

"No, thank you."

WHAT DO YOU WANT TO DO?

"Connect to a personal hard drive."

YOU DO NOT HAVE PRIVILEGES TO CONNECT TO THUNDER LORD'S HARD DRIVE.

Thunder Lord? That must be what Yves had told his 'quist to call him. Looking at the contact screen was starting to give me a blinding headache. "I don't want that hard drive. I want to connect to a different one. Please show me available drives now."

In a flash, several options popped up. It seemed I wasn't the only one with a secure hard drive. I moved my hand and scrolled down to my drive. I tapped my foot twice to access it.

"Please create a new folder."

DONE.

I searched for one name in each journal from my hard drive and highlighted it. I then dumped the selected information into the new folder.

"Please identify local nanobots."

The screen filled with scrolling information. It was like looking at a list of trillions of tiny hard drives.

"Group all nanobots into another new folder."

DONE.

Now, I just needed the 'quist to reprogram the nanobots into the shape I wanted. "Please combine the two new folders."

ACTION IS NOT PART OF PROGRAMMING. IT MUST BE PERFORMED MANUALLY.

Manually? It seemed that I would have to reprogram the nanobots all by myself.

I waved my hands around my head and turned my body as if I were dancing with the data in my hard drive.

The fake statue began to melt slightly around the edges like an ice-cream cone on a hot day. Then, after a moment, the blob lost its liquid appearance and seemed to dry out. Suddenly, particles lifted from the floor as though I had introduced a sandstorm into the room. It whirled around like a mini tornado. Out of the corner of my eye, I saw the other kids back off.

I knew that nanobots could be separated and reshaped into a new nanobot swarm projection. I felt like one of the artists I had studied as I moved my hands to sculpt and shape the swarm. Sweat dripped down my back and flew from my hands as they darted about in the air.

"Shouldn't we stop him?" I heard Charlotte ask.

Crockett shook his head.

"I'm fine," I wanted to tell her. But I didn't dare say anything that wasn't a direct command to the 'quist.

THE NANOBOTS SWARMED IN THE AIR LIKE A MINI TORNADO.

72

The mini tornado continued to spin, and I thought, I'm losing control!

I forced myself to focus all my thoughts on the one highlighted name that appeared in all the journals. The swarm of nanobots began to slow and clump together again.

Out of the whirlwind stepped the figure of a woman. She appeared to be about thirty-five years old. Her blonde hair was pulled back and she wore a simple purple dress.

Exhausted, I plucked the contact out of my eye and slumped against Crockett.

"How're you feeling?" he asked. I just nodded, unable to take my eyes off the woman.

"Who is she?" Charlotte breathed.

But I already knew the answer.

MY IDEA WORKED! JUDGE PINKERTON WAS ALIVE AGAIN!

I spent last night sitting in the hard-

backed chair between my parents' beds. Teddy slept on my lap, but I was only able to doze for a few minutes at a time. My head was too jammed with different ideas and theories about how to solve this strange mystery.

As I constantly checked to make sure that Mom and Dad's breathing hadn't changed, I felt more and more helpless. Cracking the case would be the best way I could help my parents.

But I don't think I would have been able to sleep anyway. After all, I'd never brought someone "back from the dead" like I had with Judge Pinkerton. I know that according to current definitions, Judge doesn't qualify as a true human being because she's composed of trillions and trillions of nanobots.

But she is alive.

And because Judge is a physical combination of all that my ancestors wrote about her, she has all the great qualities, smarts, and experiences listed in their different journals.

I was anxious to get cracking on the case with her, but I'd had to wait. When Judge appeared last night, she'd been as glamorous-looking as all my ancestors had said. She seemed even taller than her six feet, thanks to her straight back, upswept hairstyle, and purple heels. But she'd seemed a little shaky and had stuck out a hand to brace herself against the nearest wall.

"What's wrong with her?" I asked Crockett as we both rushed to her side.

"Once again," Crockett said, "this is brand-new territory. Not just for me but for anyone. I've never had a patient who was composed of trillions of nanobots."

"It's okay," Judge said. She regained her balance and stifled a yawn. "I think my system just needs some time to..."

"Reboot?"

"Exactly," she said with a smile. "I need to sleep for a while." She looked at me and did a double take. "You're a Fitzmorgan, aren't you?" Her eyes sparkled happily.

"Yes," I said. "But we can talk more in the morning."

We took Judge up to the Common Room, where she could lie down on a couch. We gently covered her with a blanket and, within moments, she was breathing softly. She had drifted off to sleep.

That had been seven hours ago, and I was getting more and more anxious.

I was just getting up to go check on her when the intercom near the door buzzed softly. I walked over and spoke into it. "Yes?"

"You might want to come down here." It was Crockett.

"What's up?"

"Ms. Pinkerton is awake." Crockett was the only kid without a parent along, so he had volunteered to bunk in the Common Room and keep an eye on Judge.

"I'll be right there!" I told him and hung up.

I placed Teddy on my chair. "I want you to watch Mom and Dad, Teddy." He cocked his head. "And come and find me if something happens. Okay?"

His bio-real brown eyes blinked at me twice.

"Good boy," I told him and rushed out of the room.

When I entered the Common Room, Judge was standing in front of the window. She had pulled her hair back into a loose French twist.

As if sensing I was there, she turned toward me, her expression still pensive as if she'd been considering something as she gazed outside. In a flash, her face lit up with a smile, and she walked quickly over to me.

I had a sense of déjà vu, even though I had only read about her in journals. I couldn't help but stare.

"Good morning," she said. "You must be Otis. I feel like I know you so well."

Of course she did. My own old journals were now part of her memory.

Judge grinned at me. "You look like you've seen a ghost." She laughed and tousled my hair. "Come on, let's sit down. Your friend Crockett has opened a packet of strawberry Danish. I imagine if you're anything like your relatives, you'll want one to get your brain in gear."

Crockett was already at the table, smiling at me through a mouthful of crumbs. He shrugged, as if to say, "Can you believe it?"

Judge waited until we were seated and I had started to devour a pastry. Then she asked, "Feeling better?"

"Yes, thanks," I answered. "But how about you? How do you feel?"

"Actually, I feel terrific."

"I mean, do you feel like yourself?"

She shrugged. "I don't think anyone can answer that. I feel like the me that I am now."

"Did Crockett tell you what's going on?"

"A little bit," Crockett said before she could respond.

I looked at her. "Can you help us...Judge?"

She reached out and put her hand over mine. "Nothing would make me happier. What else can you tell me about our situation?"

In careful detail, I brought her up to speed. Just as I was finishing, Lysa and Charlotte walked into the room. Lysa hesitated near the door when she saw Judge sitting with us.

"She's awake?" Lysa asked me as if Judge weren't there.

"Yes," Judge said, with a twinkle in her eye. "She is awake."

"Nice to meet you," Charlotte said and held out her hand.

"You used to train private investigators?" Lysa asked, a little suspiciously.

Before I could defend her, Judge said with a disarming smile, "That's right."

"There's nothing wrong with private investigators," Charlotte said.

"I didn't say there was," Lysa responded defensively. "I was just thinking it's a shame. I wish that we had been trained before all this. It might have been helpful now."

"I wouldn't be surprised if there was someone here who had been working on his detective skills," Charlotte said, and winked at me when no one was looking.

"How's the boy with the 'quist doing?" Judge asked, changing the subject.

78

"Yves is resting," Crockett said. "But he's growing worse. He's getting sicker quickly now, as if his body is in a race to get just as sick as the adults are. We've got to find a way to slow down the virus or kill it!"

"Which brings us back to the case," I said. "Maybe we should look harder at why ESCAPE BY A HAIR was stolen and a fake statue left in its place."

"Okay," Judge said, and I could see her mentally changing gears. "Why would someone go to all this trouble in order to get his or her hands on the real statue?"

"Well, it's very valuable, isn't it?" Lysa suggested.

"But the nanobots in me are even more valuable," Judge reminded us. "If they wanted the statue that badly, they could have saved the money they spent on the nanobots and just bid on the statue at the auction."

"I think I might know why they didn't do that," I said. "Stealing the statue was a sure way to get their hands on it. An auction wouldn't be as predictable."

Judge considered this. "How do we even know the real statue is on board?"

The memory of the 'bots moving it through the door of the Climber played in my mind. "I watched the real statue being loaded onto the Elevator," I said. "I'm positive it's here somewhere."

"But the statue is enormous," Judge considered. "Where would you hide something that large?"

Then we both looked at each other as if the same thought had hit us at the same time.

"Exactly," I said. Judge and I got up from the table together. "Come on," I said to the others.

"Where are we going?" Crockett asked.

"Down to Level 1. But first I have to stop by my room."

Once again, we squeezed through the crack in the doorway to the Control Room on Level 1. I took a seat in the Controller's chair, and the others gathered behind me.

"See this?" I pointed to one of the screens with various graphs and chang-ing numbers. "This is part of the water, air, and heating systems. If these systems went offline, we wouldn't be able to survive. All right?"

They nodded, and Judge indicated I should continue.

"Well, the computer has a way of figuring out how much weight is on the Climber so it can calculate how much oxygen and energy we'll need for our trip."

"Okay," Charlotte said. "Is this going to start making sense soon?"

"Look at this." I pointed at the condition report I had written for ESCAPE BY A HAIR, which I'd stopped to pick up from my room. "See how much the statue weighs?"

"Yes, we see," Charlotte said, sounding impatient.

"Now look at this," I said, pointing at the master report I had made. "This is how much the cargo that was loaded onto Level 5 weighs."

"But the numbers don't match up," Crockett said.

A light went on in Charlotte's eyes. "There's 650 extra pounds in the storage area!"

"That would seem to indicate that the real statue is in the storage area on Level 5. The bad guy must have hidden it there while we were still at the Elevator terminal but after I stamped it."

Judge clapped me on the back. "Bully for you, Otis! But why would someone hide it there? There's no way to access that level from inside the Elevator."

"I don't know," I said, turning the Controller's chair so that I was facing them. "But I do know we're running out of time. We're going to be on Earth in just two days."

"What about surveillance cameras?" Charlotte asked. "Can't you take a peek at Level 5 with one of those?"

"All the cameras were knocked out with the communications system. There's no way to check remotely. And since we can't get to Level 5 from inside, it looks like we won't know for sure until we get to Earth."

Crockett leaned against the airlock and tapped a finger against his lips. "I have a problem with this," he told us. "You said the bad guy must be on the Climber because he destroyed our communications system, right?"

I nodded. "That's right."

"Then why put the statue where he or she can't get at it?"

"I don't know," I replied. "But that leads to the same old question: Where is the bad guy hiding? I mean, assuming it's not one of us." The last part was a little joke, but no one laughed.

"I have an idea!" Lysa held up her hand like she was in class. "Is there a way to check and compare the weight of the other four levels?"

I shook my head. "Good idea, but no. We only kept exact records of the weight for Level 5. That's where the FSA stores samples they collect from space. So they want to know exactly how

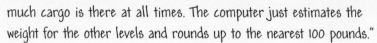

much cargo is there at all times. The computer just estimates the weight for the other levels and rounds up to the nearest 100 pounds."

Crockett seemed lost in thought. "So there's no way to prove that someone else is even on the Elevator?"

"Maybe there is," I said. "We can look for the bad guy's DNA!"

"How on Earth—or Elevator—can we do that?" Charlotte asked.

"My microprobe recognizes my DNA," I explained. "I can program it to recognize other people's DNA, as well. All I have to do is take a sample from everyone on board. Then I can run a scan level by level and see if there is any DNA that we can't account for. When we find that DNA, we might find our bad guy!"

Lysa's brow furrowed. "I don't get it."

"Think about it like this," I said. "What if I were to take everyone's fingerprints? We could look around to see if there were prints that didn't match any of ours. If we found any, they might belong to the bad guy. Well, DNA is kind of like a fingerprint. If we find some unidentified DNA, we'll know that someone else is on the Climber. Get it?"

Lysa nodded.

I removed my probe and got to work reprogramming it. Within a few minutes, I had set it up to accept more than just my DNA signature. There was enough room on the microprobe to record the DNA of hundreds of people.

"Stick out your arm," I said to Lysa.

LYSA STUCK OUT HER ARM FOR A DNA READING.

She held it out, and I placed the probe on her skin. Immediately, a chime let me know her DNA had been recorded in the probe. I labeled it with her name.

"Now every time my probe finds your DNA, it will say your name. See?" I touched the probe to her skin again, and a woman's voice said: LYSA A. BENATO.

I moved on to the other kids in the room and recorded their DNA. At this point, I wasn't analyzing anyone's DNA, just collecting it.

"What about her?" Lysa said when I was done, eyeing Judge suspiciously.

What does she have against Judge? I wondered. Did it bother her that Judge wasn't human?

"I skipped Judge for two reasons," I told Lysa. "First of all, she doesn't have DNA, and second, she wasn't even around when the communications system was destroyed."

That seemed to satisfy Lysa. I asked everyone but Crockett to go back to the Common Room and wait while we collected the DNA. I knew Charlotte and Lysa would be safe with Judge.

For the next hour, Crockett and I went from room to room on Level 4. We took the DNA of all the adults. The last person we had to get it from was Yves. His face, no longer set in a sneer, seemed to have changed. He looked almost angelic.

I was thinking about this when Crockett gave me a nudge. "All set?"

I nodded, and we left Yves's room to begin our search for the DNA of a criminal.

JUDGE WAS SITTING WITH CHARLOTTE AND LYSA.

A half hour later, Crockett and I

walked into the Common Room. Judge, Lysa, and Charlotte were sitting around a table discussing the case.

Judge was absentmindedly sketching something on a piece of paper. I heard her say, "That's one idea, Lysa. I just don't know if the criminal is an alien—" She broke off when she saw us enter. "How'd it go?" she asked eagerly.

Crockett and I looked at each other. How could we begin to tell what we had discovered?

Charlotte stood and rushed over to us. "Come on! Spill! What'd you find?"

"You'd better sit down," I told her.

"You're scaring me," she said, taking her seat again. "What happened?"

I took a deep breath before speaking. "Crockett and I went to my room first. I thought if we were going to go around invading people's property, we should start with my room. We went to my closet and ran the DNA probe over my clothes. It said my name constantly. Then I ran it over my FSA uniform, the one I was wearing when I first met you. So I wasn't surprised when my probe said your DNA was on the jacket. But I was surprised by who else's DNA was there, as well. In the exact same spot."

"Whose was it?" Charlotte asked.

"Can I show you?" I asked her.

She nodded. I placed the probe on her arm. The probe chimed and then said, CHARLOTTE NOONAN. It chimed twice more and

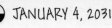

recited two more names: LYSA A. BENATO. MAXINE BENATO.

"What?" Lysa was on her feet. "Why did it say Mom's and my names? And how did our DNA get on your jacket?"

"That's just it," I answered. "Neither of you touched my jacket. But you didn't have to in order for your DNA to be on it."

"You're not making sense!" Lysa cried.

SIMPLE CLONE TESTING

So, you're going to the pet store to pick up Rover, but you want to know whether or not you're getting a clone. Just remember BONE and use the following checklist:

Bothered? Do you care if you have a clone? If not, skip the rest of the list. After all, clones deserve the same love and care as other creatures.

One of a kind? Clones are like identical twins. Do all the puppies in the litter have the exact same markings?

Need proof? A clone only needs one parent—so if the dog's papers list a mother and a father, you don't have a clone.

Extract DNA? Get a sample of the puppy's and the parent's DNA for testing. If the samples are identical, you've got a clone.

"Yes, he is," Charlotte said. "He's saying that we all have the same DNA."

Lysa swallowed. "But that would only be possible if we were..."

"If we were clones," said Charlotte, getting up again.

I'd hated springing it on Charlotte like that, but I'd needed to see her reaction. Would she be surprised? Or would she angrily deny it?

But instead, Charlotte just seemed numb. Not Lysa, though. She shouted, "Just because we look alike doesn't mean we're clones! If we were, wouldn't we be identical?"

"Not necessarily," I said. "Clones share the same DNA, but environmental things—like what you eat and where you live—can change your appearance." Lysa shook her head, not wanting to hear any more. But I had to keep going. "Lysa, your mom is decades older, so she's going to look different than you two." Then, looking

86

at Charlotte's blonde locks, I added, "And one of you has been coloring her hair."

Charlotte took a moment to speak. "Am I a suspect?" she asked quietly.

"We're all suspects," I told her.

I think my gentle tone actually made things worse. She seemed to take it as a sign of pity or something. "But I think I might have moved closer to the top of the list," she snapped. "I guess you might feel safer if I stayed in my room."

I couldn't argue with her. "Just for now, until we can get the situation straightened out. You, too, Lysa."

Charlotte grimaced as if she had tasted something awful. But she nodded and left. Lysa followed her out.

"I'll make sure they get back to their rooms," Crockett said.

LYSA AND CHARLOTTE WERE SHOCKED AND ANGRY.

I slumped into the chair where Charlotte had been sitting. Feeling frazzled, I squeezed my eyes shut and put my head in my hands. I felt Judge's hand on my shoulder. She said sympathetically, "I'm not sure if anyone could have handled that better."

With my head still down, I opened my eyes and found myself looking directly at the drawing Judge had been working on when I came in earlier.

JUDGE'S SKETCH

The sketch showed men in old-fashioned suits helping a little girl with black hair off a train. The girl looked to be about six years old—and exactly like a younger version of Lysa Benato. In the background of the drawing, I could make out a city that looked like it might be San Francisco. It was in flames.

"What's this?" I said, tapping the paper.

"Oh, that? Just a memory I had," Judge said. "It came to me while I was talking to Charlotte and Lysa. I thought maybe it was because you remind me of your ancestor Fitz."

"You mean my great-great-great-great-grandmother?" I couldn't help but laugh with the last "great."

"You remind me a lot of her," she said. "And that's quite a compliment."

"Thanks, Judge." For some reason, I couldn't take my eyes off the drawing.

Judge noticed and said, "You can keep it if you like."

"I'd love it," I told her. "But maybe you should give it to Lysa since you drew a younger version of her in the picture."

"That's not Lysa," Judge said. "That's Asyla Notabe."

I looked up, surprised. "You mean the Asyla Notabe who started the campaign against private detectives?"

"That's right," Judge said. "Even she was a little girl at one point. In fact, I met her in 1906 on the same train that I met Fitz. We were on our way to San Francisco."

"That's the answer," I said. "It's been right there the whole time!"

"What is it?"

I quickly wrote out the three names.

CHARLOTTE NOONAN
MAXINE BENATO
LYSA A. BENATO

"Do you see it?" I said. "I know you and my family worked on anagrams to crack many cases together. And it looks like this one might hinge on anagrams, too."

"What do you mean?" asked Judge. She gazed at the names for a moment. "Benato is an anagram for Notabe!"

"Look at Lysa's full name."

LYSA A. BENATO

I rearranged the letters until they spelled:

ASYLA NOTABE

I pushed the paper toward Judge. "Lysa A. Benato is an anagram for Asyla Notabe!"

"You're right!" Judge cried. "But what about Charlotte Noonan? She's a clone, as well, but her name isn't even close to an anagram."

I tapped the pen thoughtfully against the table. "That's true. And why would there be three Notabe clones on this Climber, anyway? Does it have to do with ESCAPE BY A HAIR? And does the person who took the statue know how to stop the virus?"

89

"Well," Judge said, "there might be one way to answer some of our questions. We can talk to Lysa and Charlotte."

LYSA DIDN'T SEEM TO TRUST JUDGE.

Lysa wasn't in her room, so we checked her mom's. Mrs. Benato was lying in bed asleep, and Lysa was sitting in a chair next to the bed watching over her.

When she saw Judge, Lysa said, "No offense, but for some reason you make me nervous."

Judge didn't take offense at Lysa's comment the way I might have. Instead, she gave Lysa a little smile. "Why don't I wait outside?"

Before I could protest, Judge left the room. The door slid shut behind her, and I turned to Lysa. I was angry. "You're going to have to get used to constructed intelligent life."

"Am I?" she asked, seeming genuinely surprised by my anger. "You mean there are more of them?"

"People might consider you prejudiced." I was going against all my training by being hostile to a potential witness.

"Prejudiced!" Lysa spat back at me. Traces of the mousy girl slipped away as she grew more frazzled. "Are you honestly here to insult me? Let's just cut to the chase. In case you haven't noticed, my mom is knocked out and lying sick in bed. Do you think I'd ever do anything to endanger her life?"

Lysa's face was red, and there were tears pooling in her eyes.

"No," I answered. "I guess you're right. I'm sorry."

"Doesn't that fact clear me of suspicion?" she asked angrily.

"Again, I'm sorry," I said. "I just have one question: Why are you and your mom on the Climber?"

"Two tickets were e-mailed to us. The note said we had won first prize in a sweepstakes. My mom and I couldn't remember entering any sweepstakes—but we decided not to ask too many questions. The tickets were real, and who wouldn't want a free ride on the Space Elevator?"

I opened my mouth, but she interrupted me. "Before you ask who sent them, I don't know. The e-mail is gone. It's been erased. Satisfied?"

Without waiting for me to respond, she said, "I'd like you to leave now."

I nodded and left the room. Judge was waiting for me outside the door.

"That didn't go so well," I told her.

"I know," she said. "I could hear it all. Now what?"

"Let's try Charlotte."

If it's possible, that interview went even worse. In fact, there really wasn't an interview.

When we knocked on Charlotte's door, we heard her muffled voice say, "Go away!"

"Charlotte, I just want to ask you one or two questions," I called. "Did someone send you tickets for the Elevator?"

"They came in an e-mail. They were prizes in a sweepstakes."

"What sweepstakes?"

"I don't know," she answered. "I figured my dad had entered and forgotten about doing it."

My brain went into hyperdrive. Clearly, the sweepstakes
had been a fake. Someone…the thief…was trying to throw a
potential investigation off-track by having so many people with the
same DNA located in one place.

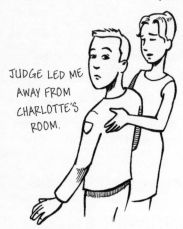

JUDGE LED ME
AWAY FROM
CHARLOTTE'S
ROOM.

Before I could shout another
question through the door,
Charlotte bellowed, "NOW…
GO…AWAY!"

"Come on," Judge said, gently
pulling me back toward the elevator.

"Well, we're getting nowhere,"
I said. "There's no one else to ask."

"I think there might be, Otis."

"Who?"

"Asyla Notabe."

Once again, Judge and I were in the Common Room. Crockett
was seated at the table, watching us pace back and forth. We had
just filled him in on our progress.

"I think it's a great idea to bring Asyla to life the way you
brought me back," Judge said. "Then we can ask her questions
about her clones and find out if she knows anything about what
they might be up to."

"It won't be the real Asyla," I replied. "It will only be the woman
as my family's written about her in their journals. And the journals
say much more about you than about her."

"If you added other information in your hard drive—like news
stories or encyclopedias—she should still be well rounded." Judge
stopped pacing and looked at me. "What's the real reason you're
hesitating?"

I took a breath. "I'm concerned about what will happen to you."

"It's true." Judge acknowledged. "We will have to use some of the nanobots I'm made of."

Crockett chimed in, "If we do that, you'll have to be younger and smaller."

"What do you mean?" I asked.

"Think about the nanobots that make up Judge like the sand in a sand castle," Crockett explained. "If you want to make a second castle using the same sand, the first one will have to get smaller."

"So I'll have to be younger and less experienced," Judge said. "But it still might work."

I stopped pacing. "Are you sure you want to do this, Judge?"

Judge stood still. "Honestly, it's scares me a little. But I'm not sure what else to do."

"Okay," I finally agreed. "Let's bring Asyla Notabe back."

But before we got started, I had to do one thing. I went to the kitchen area of the room and found an apple. I placed it on a table in front of Judge.

"What's this for?" she asked.

"I'm going to force the nanobots we take from you through this apple before they take the shape of Asyla," I said.

Crockett looked at me like I was nuts. "But why?"

"It's a kind of insurance," I said. "Let's just hope we never need it. Do you still have Yves's contact?"

He nodded and got the glass that contained the contact lenses.

"Everyone ready?" I asked. They both nodded, and I popped one of the contacts into my eye.

HELLO, OTIS, Yves's 'quist said in my mind. WHAT WOULD YOU LIKE TO DO?

I explained my goal to the 'quist and got to work. My hands danced and my body moved about. Once again, the air was filled with flying nanobots.

More than half the nano-material flew off Judge, zoomed through the apple, and reorganized into the shape of... my math teacher!

RECIPES FOR ROBOTS
COOKING FOR YOUR 'BOTS

What's a chef to do when the nanobots are hungry and there's nothing in the cupboard? Reach for the garbage!

1) The new nanobots might be hungry all the time, but they're not picky! They can adapt to stimuli such as heat, light, sounds, surface textures, chemicals, and disgusting food. Feed 'em scraps from the trash – they won't complain.

2) Looking for the perfect meal? Any sugary food will do. WARNING: Foods high in glucose, such as fruits and some vegetables, may also attract bacteria that could interfere with the operation of your nanobots.

3) Feed the 'bots on your schedule. Don't let them run your life. Remember, they can go for months without eating. But when you do give them a meal, watch out! The feeding frenzy can be frightening!

Judge looked smaller—and extremely concerned as she asked, "What's happened?"

I wondered the same thing. Why had I been thinking of my math teacher?

Judge's eyes narrowed. "Are you concentrating?"

"Sorry!" I shouted, and refocused my mind.

My math teacher disintegrated as the nanobots flew apart into a whirling dervish of technology. The cloud of 'bots expanded and constricted almost as if it were breathing. Then it constricted one final time into the shape of a tall woman.

She looked to be about twenty-nine years old and was shockingly beautiful.

"Are you Asyla Notabe?" I asked.

She stroked her long black hair, seeming to relish the feel of the silky strands. "Ooooh…it's good to be back."

Asyla took a step toward Judge, who now looked to be about nine years old, the same age she would have been when she met Fitz Morgan in 1906. Towering over her, Asyla eyed Judge for a moment like a spider about to devour her prey.

She staggered then. Her hand lashed out and her fingers closed around my upper arm. Hard. The strength of the nanobots was incredible.

I grimaced but managed not to call out.

ASYLA NOTABE

95

"Hmmm..." Asyla looked as if she were savoring a delicious meal. I couldn't shake free of her grasp.

"Let him go," Judge said, stepping forward.

"Yes. I have to sleep now," Asyla said and released my arm. Crockett and I helped her over to the couch.

Almost instantly, Asyla went to sleep so that her system could reboot.

"Otis, are you okay?" Judge was gazing at me as if looking for injuries.

I nodded. "I'm fine, but what about you? How do you feel, Judge?"

JUDGE LOOKED ABOUT NINE YEARS OLD.

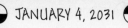

She looked down at her simple purple dress and her small body. "A little strange."

"Are you starting to have doubts about bringing Asyla back?"

But Judge didn't answer me. She just looked down at Asyla sleeping quietly on the couch.

And all the while, our doomed Elevator continued to plummet toward Earth.

ASYLA WAS MORE INTERESTED IN HER REFLECTION THAN THE VIEW!

I awoke this morning with a start.

There wasn't time for sleep! We had to hunt down the bad guy!

It took me a second to realize where I was. The sharp kink in my neck helped remind me. I was in my parents' room. I had slept in the chair between their beds again.

My eyes instantly went to them. Their IV packs were dripping away. They were breathing steadily, but their pulse rate was still really high.

Teddy clicked and whirled, looking up at me with concern.

"It's okay, Teddy," I told him, but I don't think sounded very convincing. Teddy's eyes didn't change, and he kept watching me.

I told him to watch over Mom and Dad and headed out the door. Judge had sent me to bed last night, telling me not to worry, she would stay with Asyla. The first item on today's agenda was to check in on them.

At the door of the Common Room, I heard the sound of voices.

"Don't you just love this?" It was Asyla speaking. She was standing in front of the window, and I saw that she wasn't admiring the view. Instead, she was gazing at her own reflection.

When I entered, I was once again struck by how small Judge looked standing next to Asyla. I hoped we had made the right decision in bringing her back.

Judge rolled her eyes toward Asyla when she saw me. "It seems some things never change. Can we get to work now, Asyla?"

Asyla touched her hair, as if savoring the feel of it. "Oh, I'm not here to work, little girl." She stressed the word little. "That would mean I'd have to be paid."

"Money isn't such an issue anymore," I told her.

She didn't turn away from her reflection. "There's always something to be paid."

I thought about the sacrifice Judge had made to bring Asyla back. "How about life?" I asked. "Is that enough of a payment?"

"What are you saying? You're going to destroy me unless I answer your questions?" She chuckled. "I don't think so. Not if you're like the Fitzmorgans I remember."

"Fine, can we just chat? Please?" I forced myself to whine slightly. And it worked. The begging tone in my voice seemed to satisfy her.

"Very well." She finally turned from her reflection and glided over to a chair. She perched on the edge, as if this arrangement could change at any time. "What is it you want to talk about? My old friend Justine has told me all about your situation. Quite a pickle you've gotten yourself into. Seems like the rest of us are always cleaning up Fitzmorgan and Moorie messes."

ASYLA SEEMED
WILLING
TO TALK.

That's not true! I wanted to shout. But instead, I asked, "Can you tell us about the statue?"

"Statue?" her voice remained calm, but she looked interested.

"That's one thing I didn't tell you about, Asyla," Judge said.

Asyla ignored her. "What statue?"

I looked at Judge and nodded. She said, "It's a work by Maginold Moylan that's gone missing. We think it might be somewhere on the Climber."

I saw a flash of excitement in Asyla's eyes.

"Seems there might be something we know about that would interest you," I said. "Let's strike a deal, Asyla. If you answer a few of our questions, we'll answer yours."

She waved a hand at me as if sweeping the idea from the air. "Even if there was a statue that once caught my eye, why would I tell you about it?"

Judge replied, "Because all of our problems seem to have started with that statue."

"And because your clones are on this Climber," I added. "And they might die unless we get to the truth."

"Yes, darling Justine told me all about my 'relatives' on this Elevator," Asyla said. "How wonderful to be surrounded by such fine company! I'm not worried about them. They must have a plan."

I shook my head. "I don't think so. Mrs. Benato is unconscious and infected with the virus. She's growing sicker by the hour."

That seemed to reach Asyla. "Describe the statue to me," she said. Was she going to cooperate? "If you do, I'll tell you what I can. No more cat-and-mouse games. I think we've established who the mice are in the room, anyway."

I looked at Judge, who shrugged. What did we have to lose?

I described the scene the statue portrayed: Mary Todd Lincoln stretching out a hand toward Lincoln's killer, John Wilkes Booth, her fingers just barely missing him. "It's called ESCAPE BY A HAIR."

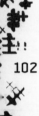

Asyla's eyes gleamed at the name. "ESCAPE BY A HAIR," she repeated slowly. And there was something about the way she stretched out the last word...

Then her eyes went cold again. She shook her head. "I've never heard of it."

You didn't have to be a detective to know she was lying.

Judge suddenly said, "It's the title, isn't it? That's what made you sit up straighter."

No answer for a moment, and then Asyla laughed. "Of course not. I don't even know what that silly name means."

But it seemed Judge was on to something.

"ESCAPE BY A HAIR," I said, thinking out loud, stretching out the last word the way Asyla had. I remembered the list of materials used to make the statue: tin, marble—and human hair.

Yes! That must be it!

"This all has something to do with the hair inside the statue, doesn't it?" I asked Asyla.

She turned her gaze on me, and it was like looking into the eye of a hurricane. Cool, barely controlled rage stared back at me. Besides sending a shiver down my spine, it told me we were on the right track.

Then Asyla blinked, and the rage disappeared, hidden behind a mask of calm innocence. She opened her mouth, and I thought she might speak. Instead, she yawned and stretched. "Oh my, I'm sleepy," she said.

Asyla walked to the couch and curled up on it, letting her long black hair drape over the end like a dark curtain. "I'm afraid we'll have to talk about this another time," she purred. "Unless you're going to force me to stay awake. But that would be inhumane."

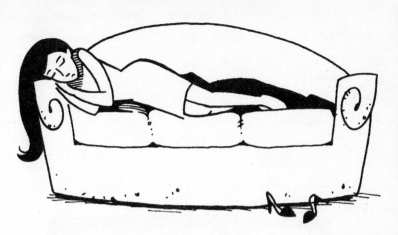

Before we could protest, she closed her eyes. Judge took a step toward her as if she wanted to shake her awake, but stopped herself.

We shared a look, and I shrugged helplessly. Judge and I left the room and stood in the hallway next to the elevator.

"What did you think of that?" Judge asked me.

I shook my head. "She definitely knows something, but I don't know what."

"Or she could be playing a game with us, making us believe she has knowledge we want," Judge offered. "She might be as in the dark as we are."

"The way she reacted to the title of the statue," I said. "It must have something to do with the hair."

"Okay," Judge agreed. "But what?"

I thought for a second. "The hair...the hair..."

I couldn't finish the sentence. What could be so important about hair in the statue?

I DREAMED MY MATH TEACHER WAS SHOUTING AT ME.

Last night I dreamed of my math

teacher. The dreams were more like nightmares, really. She kept flashing my grade on my desk video screen. F. F. F.

"You didn't do the work!" she shouted over and over. "You have the answer, but you didn't do the work!"

When I woke with a start, my body was drenched in sweat.

Of course, the dream was my subconscious telling me that I was letting everyone down. And I mean everyone: The kids on the Elevator, my parents...the entire planet!

Outside my window, space was just as dark, but Earth was now much bigger. We're almost out of time! I thought. Any moment now, the virus will become airborne. We'll breathe it in, and then we'll be just like the adults. And when we reach Earth's surface at the end of the day...

When I went to check on my parents, I found Crockett just leaving their room. If it were possible, he looked even more tired than before. The bags under his wide eyes looked like permanent black tattoos.

"Any change?" I asked him.

He nodded grimly. "Yes, but not a good one. Your parents and the other adults are getting worse, Otis. I don't know what I can do." He put a hand on my shoulder. "I'm sorry."

I went into my parents' room and sat with them for a while.

Teddy clicked and clacked and did a small, subdued leap when he saw me. He crawled into his favorite spot in my jacket pocket, where he curled up contentedly. But I didn't feel relaxed. Something was nagging at me. Something about math...

After tucking their blankets securely around my mom and dad, I returned to my own room. For the second time during this horrible journey, I took out the Condition Reports that I had created for the works of art.

I ran my eyes carefully over the reports for a few minutes. I was just thinking that maybe I was on the wrong track after all—when I spotted it! Of course! The answer to all the mysteries was waiting for us on Level 5.

Not only was the missing statue there, but also the bad guy!

I would need help to go up there.

Judge had to keep an eye on Asyla. Crockett couldn't go. He needed to be close to the patients. Lysa was an option, but I could think of someone even better.

CHARLOTTE PEERED OUT AT ME.

I rushed out of my room and down the hall to Charlotte's door. I knocked.

"What?" her muffled voice asked.

"It's me," I called.

"Me who?"

"Charlotte, please open the door."

She called back, "Aren't you worried about my being an evil clone? Aren't you scared that I'll attack you?"

"I need your help. The bad guy is on Level 5, and we need to go up there now."

There was silence. Then I heard her say, "D'en. Just a crack, computer." The door slid open several inches, and Charlotte peered out at me. "You need

help? So you're here because you
have no one else to go to?"

"No," I said. "I'm here because
I don't want to go to anyone else."

"Right," she said sarcastically.

"I'm serious."

She studied my face. And
what she saw there made her
anger recede. She stepped back
and said, "D'en, computer." The
door slid the rest of the way open,
and she said, "Come on in."

I followed her over to the couch, past her father, who was
snoring gently in his bed. "How is he?"

"Crockett told me he's getting worse," she said, tears welling
up in her eyes.

"I might be on to a way to help him and the rest of the adults."

She looked at me. "You trust me enough to tell me about
your plan?"

"Yes," I said.

Charlotte seemed to understand I really meant it. She gestured
for me to take a seat on the couch and sat next to me.

She took a breath and started speaking. "When I was a baby, my
real mom and dad died. A kindly neighbor took me in. It was Robert
Noonan. He adopted me, and I changed my last name to his."

"That's why your last name isn't an anagram for Notabe."

She nodded. "Judge came here last night and told me all about
that. Just so you know, I had no idea I was a clone until yesterday.
I changed my hair color from black to blonde for fun, that's all.

Not because I was trying to trick anyone... especially you."

As she said "you," her eyes met mine. And for the first time, I felt like we were really seeing each other. A long moment passed.

"So...," she broke the silence. "How do you know the bad guy is on Level 5?"

"I dreamed my math teacher was trying to tell me something," I said. "She kept saying, 'You have the answer.' Remember how we figured out that there are 650 pounds on Level 5 that shouldn't be there?"

"Sure," she said, nodding. "That's because the real statue is probably on that level. Or do you think it's somewhere else now?"

I shook my head. "No, it's there. I know it. But I went over my notes again. The statue only weighs 510 pounds. That leaves a difference of 140 pounds." I showed her the Condition Report for ESCAPE BY A HAIR.

Realization dawned on her face. "Which means there is something—"

"Or someone. Someone who weighs 140 pounds and is hiding on Level 5."

"But how would the bad guy get there?" she asked.

108

"He probably used the airlock hatch in the Control Room to get outside the Climber and make his way to Level 5."

Charlotte's face showed her excitement. "Now it makes sense! That's why the Controller's body was slumped toward the airlock in the Control Room. Someone had opened that door to get to the outside. When they did, the change of pressure tugged the Controller in the direction of the door."

I nodded. "You're right. I've looked at plans of the Climber. There's a work ladder that runs along the outside of it from Level 1 to Level 5."

"You're going to make the trip?"

I nodded.

"You wouldn't dive into the depths of the ocean without a buddy, would you? Why should this be any different? I'm going with you."

"Are you sure, Charlotte?"

"I've been locked up in my room for the past two days," she said. "If you think you're going to lock me out of this, you've got another thing coming."

Charlotte and I headed for the Common Room, where we found Judge. "I'll go," she said immediately after I brought her up to speed.

I shook my head. "Charlotte and I have it covered."

When the three of us got to the Control Room on Level 1, we forced open the closet that held the emergency Extra

JUDGE VOLUNTEERED TO GO.

Vehicular Activity (EVA) suits. The space suits looked like clear plastic jumpsuits. The hard, plastic helmets were the only parts of the outfit that were inflexible. They also contained the monitors. The closet had places for three space suits—but there were only two.

ONE SPACE SUIT WAS MISSING.

"The bad guy must have taken the third suit," Charlotte said, and I nodded.

"I really should be the one to go to Level 5," Judge said. "The trip would be so short my cells could make the trip without any extra oxygen. I wouldn't have to wear a mask. And I'm stronger than you. I'll prove it," she added with a smile. "Want to arm wrestle?"

I smiled back but shook my head. "That's exactly why you can't go. Someone equal in strength to Asyla needs to stay here."

"Crockett and Lysa are keeping an eye on her for the moment. Asyla seems content to sit and stare at her own reflection," Judge said. "Besides, I'm afraid she might actually be stronger than I am."

"Still, if something goes wrong, we wouldn't be any match for her," I said. "You're the only one who'd even have a chance."

For a minute, I thought we might witness Judge's famous stubborn streak. But then I saw her face change. "You're right," she finally said. "I don't like it and I hate to miss out on this, but you're right."

"Sorry, Judge," I said softly.

She gave me a smile. "We'll have more adventures to share, I'm sure," she said. "Well, now that that's decided, I'd better go back and relieve Crockett and Lysa." Judge reached up and tousled my hair and then Charlotte's. "Good luck, you two."

The space suits were much easier to move around in than I had expected, and Charlotte and I had no problem making our way outside. The airlock had two hatches. One opened from the Control Room into a small room. Another hatch opened from there to the outside.

Once we had closed the first hatch behind us,

CHARLOTTE STEPPED ONTO THE LEDGE.

we waited a second for the room to depressurize. Then we opened the outside hatch—and stepped carefully onto the small ledge and into the darkness of space. I had to duck under the lowest rung of the steel ladder that ran up the side of the Climber. A flexible steel cable was connected at one end to Charlotte's suit and ran through a clip in my suit. I attached the opposite end of the cable to the bottom rung of the ladder.

There are only a few hundred people in the world who can say that they've gone on a space walk. And now Charlotte and I could be added to the list. Out there, there was no artificial gravity. We

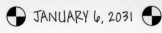

would have floated off into space if we hadn't been holding on to the handles on the outside of the hatch.

I could feel and hear the workings of the magnetic clamps on the other side of the Climber as they grabbed onto the ribbon and lowered us down. But if I hadn't known we were descending, I wouldn't have been able to feel it.

Not that I paid much attention to anything but the view. Imagine floating above Earth with nothing but a clear plastic helmet and space between you and the planet. It was a rush like I'd never had before.

I felt something bump against me. It was Charlotte. She placed her hand in mine. I looked up, thinking something was wrong. We weren't able to talk to each other—the communication equipment on the suits wasn't working. It must have been tied in with the system on the Climber.

Charlotte gestured toward Earth with her head and then looked back at me, her eyes wide, as if to say, "I can't believe how beautiful this is!"

STEPPING OUTSIDE THE ELEVATOR AND SEEING EARTH WAS AMAZING!

Her hand stayed in mine for a second longer. Then it was time to climb up the ladder. Charlotte went first. We both moved very carefully, keeping one hand on a rung as the other hand reached for the next one up. The lack of gravity and the feeling of being nearly weightless reminded me of swimming.

As we climbed up, we passed windows set into the thick, smooth steel of the Climber. As we passed the windows for Level 3, I looked inside, hoping to catch a glimpse of Judge, Crockett, or Asyla. But none of the windows gave a view of the Common Room.

We were nearly to our destination. The windows to Level 4 were now on the other side of the ladder. Just a few more feet—

CRACK!

Suddenly, Charlotte was floating away from the Climber, a broken rung still in her hand! Somehow, it must have snapped off the ladder.

Instinctively, I reached for her.

My fingertips brushed against her suit, but I missed. I strained harder to grab her, and I lost my grip on the rung.

Now I was floating right behind Charlotte.

She managed to turn around so we could see each other's faces. I tried to give her a reassuring look. We would be okay, I wanted to say. We're still connected to the ladder by the cable. We just have to pull ourselves back to the Climber.

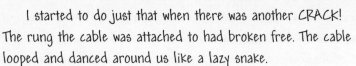

I started to do just that when there was another CRACK! The rung the cable was attached to had broken free. The cable looped and danced around us like a lazy snake.

Now Charlotte and I were both moving away from the Climber—out into space.

Charlotte's eyes widened. If I panicked now, I knew we'd be lost. Every single second counted.

I quickly formulated a plan. I pulled on the cable that still connected me to Charlotte until we were bumping up against each other. I managed to turn our bodies so that I was facing the Climber and she had her back to it.

She looked at me like I was crazy.

"Kick off me!" I mouthed. "Do it!"

She understood. Her face lost some of its panic as she held onto my shoulders and brought up her feet so they were pressed against my lower chest.

114

Then, as if I were a springboard, Charlotte pushed off from me. Her feet dug into my suit, and I prayed that it wouldn't rip. Then she was drifting quickly back toward the Elevator.

She gripped the side of the ladder this time, not the rungs.

CHARLOTTE PULLED ME BACK.

Once she had one arm looped around the ladder, she slowly reeled me back in like a giant fish.

"Good work, Charlotte!" I shouted, even though I knew she couldn't hear me.

I took a quick look at where the broken rungs had connected to the sides of the ladder. The bottom half of each remaining nub was rough, but the top half was smooth. It was clear that someone had filed halfway through the rungs. Someone had sabotaged the ladder to keep from being followed.

If Charlotte hadn't come with me, I probably would have been lost in space.

Charlotte had paused to look at the broken rungs as well. Our eyes met, and I mouthed, "Thank you."

She gave me a harried smile and mouthed, "Let's go."

We couldn't take a chance that any more of the rungs had been filed, but we could still climb up to Level 5 and return later by pulling ourselves along the sides of the ladder.

A few minutes later, we had finished our climb. Luckily, there was no way to lock the hatch for the airlock from the inside. We tumbled through the outer door and into the small depressurizing chamber.

116

OUR ONLY LIGHT CAME FROM THE FINGERTIPS OF OUR GLOVES.

I held a finger in front of my mouth

to indicate that we should be quiet.

Charlotte shrugged and pulled a face, and I knew what she meant. Our entrance through the airlock must have made enough racket to alert anyone on the level that someone had entered.

A thin strip on the sleeve of my suit glowed green, indicating that there was now oxygen in the chamber. We quickly unsnapped our helmets and set them silently down on the floor.

As we opened the inner hatch, my ears were filled with the loud hum of working machinery. Much of the mechanical equipment that ran the magnetic clamps was housed on this level. I could only hope that noise had been enough to cover our entrance.

The lights were off and the space was dark, but I knew it held stacks of boxes, large crates, and pieces of scientific equipment as well as most of the artworks from the auction. I didn't dare call for lights, knowing that they would give us away to whoever was hiding here. The working lights on the fingertips of our suits would have to be enough. We were forced to walk like zombies, our hands stretched out in front of us as we shuffled forward as quietly as we could.

"Otis," Charlotte breathed into my ear, startling me. I turned and raised my eyebrows, as if to say, What's up?

She fluttered her fingers. The fingertip lights had started to dim. I looked at my own fingers, and saw those lights were fading, as well. Too late, I realized that the batteries for the lights must be housed in the helmets. Soon we would be plunged into total darkness. But we had come too far. We couldn't turn back now.

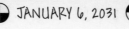

"Let's just look a little longer," I whispered in her ear as quietly as I could. She nodded, and we continued working our way through the crates. It grew darker and darker.

I turned to look at Charlotte just before the lights went out. She was shaking her hands, like you might shake a flashlight, as if that might make the lights stay on longer. But the lights dimmed even more and then died. The last thing I saw was her wide, frightened eyes. "Oh, no," she whispered.

I pulled off my gloves and reached out to take her hand... and felt nothing.

There was no one there. She must have wandered away from me in the darkness.

I risked a whisper. "Charlotte?"

No answer. We were now separated. One of my groping hands bumped into something sharp. Very sharp. I pulled back my hand and sucked on my fingers. The skin hadn't been broken.

What on Earth had I just touched?

Of course! SHARP TEETH!

I remembered that I had asked the 'bot to store the artwork on Level 5 to keep it from hurting anyone. I never dreamed that I might find myself being the one it hurt!

I was just about to move along when I smelled petunias.

It's said that smells create the strongest memories. And, at least in my case, it's totally true. As the petunia-scented perfume struck my olfactory nerve, a vivid image flashed into my mind. I saw Ms. Jenkins, the customs guard, grabbing my jacket and spinning me around.

My mind zoomed in on part of the image. I watched her fingers as they closed around my arm. They landed on the exact spot where I'd found the DNA that matched that of Charlotte, Lysa, and Mrs. Benato.

My probe should have picked up different DNA for Ms. Jenkins, even though it wouldn't have been able to match it to a name since I hadn't recorded it.

But it had only picked up DNA for the three clones.

Ms. Jenkins must be yet another clone of Asyla Notabe!

I was thunderstruck. It seemed there was an army of them. Only Ms. Jenkins must be the bad guy we were looking for! She was perfectly placed to switch the statues. After I had instructed the worker 'bots to load the real statue onto Level 2, Ms. Jenkins could have told the 'bots to take the real statue to Level 5 instead. Then she must have set up the fake statue on Level 2. She could easily move about the Climber with her security clearance.

I had to find Charlotte and tell her of my discovery.

But I was too late.

"Lights!" The cry echoed off the walls, and the room blazed with light.

It took a moment for my eyes to adjust to the glare. But I wasn't surprised to find Ms. Jenkins standing there, her hands on her hips like a mighty conqueror. She took off

IT WAS MS. JENKINS!

119

Buy the **KNIGHT 3400** Night Goggle System Now!

If your night vision goggles are interfering with your 'quist transmissions, try the KNIGHT 3400 system. In dim light, KNIGHT 3400 converts light particles into electrons, which strike and create an image on a screen—just like your basic night goggles.

However, in total darkness, the KNIGHT 3400 uses ultraviolet radiation to light the room instead of an infrared flashlight, which blocks 'quist transmissions. Like infrared, ultraviolet light is invisible, but it won't mess with your 'quist!

And that's not all! Old screens were green and hazy, but the KNIGHT 3400 comes with a full-color, crystal clear viewer!

WARNING! All orders must be made through proper government channels!

120

the night goggles she'd been wearing and tossed them to the floor. Clearly, she had been using them to watch us stumble around in the dark. Behind her was the real ESCAPE BY A HAIR statue.

"I should've known you'd be trouble," she hissed as she strode toward me.

I moved quickly, pulled my probe out of my belt loop, and turned to SHARP TEETH.

"What are you doing?" she asked. "You think your little artworks can save you?"

"Yes," I said, connecting the SHARP TEETH battery wires to my probe. "Actually, I do."

Ms. Jenkins said, "Ha!" like any good villain, and continued toward me.

Now! I thought, and flicked the switch on my probe.

Instantly, it acted like a battery and sent power into SHARP TEETH. The giant jaws immediately started chattering. They bounced off the crate they'd been sitting on and clattered across the floor, heading straight for Ms. Jenkins.

But the teeth were moving too slowly. Ms. Jenkins just glanced down at them and laughed. She easily stepped out of the way, and the teeth rammed into a stack of large boxes behind her and started gnawing away at the bottom one.

"Nice try," she said, tossing back her jet-black hair and giving me a twisted grin.

She started advancing toward me slowly, and I tried desperately to keep my eyes from watching SHARP TEETH.

THE BOXES CAME TUMBLING DOWN.

Just as her shadow fell over me and her body blocked out everything else, I heard a crunching sound. SHARP TEETH had torn through the side of the box, and it caved in under the weight of the boxes above. The entire stack teetered and began to lean...

Ms. Jenkins turned just in time to see the boxes start to fall. She raised her arms to protect her head, as they came crashing down all around her. She howled in rage as asteroid samples tumbled out of one of the boxes and fell on her, pinning her to the ground.

121

18 - SCIENCE ALLIANCE MAGAZINE

SPACE ROCKS

Taking a trip on the Space Elevator? Be sure to check out the asteroid samples on display at the top. If these asteroids hadn't been snatched out of space, they might have reached Earth someday.

When asteroids enter Earth's atmosphere, they and the streaks of light they make as they burn up are called meteors (commonly known as shooting stars). Over a million meteors bombard the atmosphere every day—and every once and awhile, one is big enough to make it to Earth's surface. Then it's called a meteorite.

One of the biggest smashed into Earth about 65 million years ago and may have caused the extinction of the dinosaurs. But not to worry—a new state-of-the-art detection system gives us time to redirect or destroy a large asteroid well before it endangers Earth.

"Let me go!" she screamed. Clearly, nothing was wrong with her lungs, and she looked uninjured. I decided it was safe to leave her there for a second.

"I will," I told her. "But first I have some questions for you."

"Make that WE have some questions." It was Charlotte, and she was coming around the side of a large crate.

"Hello, little sister," Ms. Jenkins purred. "You're just in time to help me."

Charlotte just glared at her. "You're not my sister. I may be your clone, but I don't know you."

122

She walked toward me. I was glad to see her, and we exchanged relieved smiles. We had found the bad guy and subdued her. Now if we could just get her to tell how us how to destroy the virus, everything would be fine.

"This was all your doing, wasn't it?" I asked her. "You e-mailed the tickets to your clones to come on board the Elevator. You wanted to confuse any possible investigation into the stolen statue."

Ms. Jenkins didn't respond, but I could see from her eyes that I was right.

Charlotte took a step toward her. "How could you invite your own flesh and blood onto this Climber and then infect them with a deadly virus?"

Ms. Jenkins remained silent for a moment and then said, "I never wanted to use the virus. It was just my emergency plan, in case something went wrong. And you," she added bitterly, pointing at me with her one free hand, "you went wrong."

"How?" I asked. "By discovering that the statue on Level 2 was a fake?"

The guard laughed. "I was in the Control Room when you were on Level 2. I saw you on one of the cameras, and when I heard you say that the statue was a fake, I triggered the attack. I thought my plan was ruined when the elevator stopped on Level 3 and that Yves Jackson spotted me. But everything kept running along smoothly. Until now."

Charlotte shook her head. "How could you do this to anyone—especially to people you call 'sister'?"

"Don't be so melodramatic!" Ms. Jenkins cried. "That virus has a built-in timer. It will die within the next twenty-four hours. I just needed everyone out of the way for a while. Unfortunately, I forgot that children under eighteen wouldn't have 'quists and wouldn't be infected. Besides, the hair inside that statue was worth all the risks. I needed to have time alone with it so I could use a laser tool and extract the hair without noticeably harming the statue. I didn't want you or other art experts to notice that the hair was gone. I thought I would be able to do it without getting caught."

I was opening my mouth to ask her more about the hair when something moved in the corner of my vision. I turned just for a split second. It was Judge! What was she doing here?

Ms. Jenkins took advantage of the distraction and tried to push herself up out of the broken boxes and asteroid samples. She freed her other arm, but that's as far as she got. Her movements disturbed another stack of boxes that had been leaning precariously, and they tumbled down on top of her.

123

Only Ms. Jenkins's head was poking out of the pile, and she was unconscious. I could see now that she was wearing a prosthetic nose. The fake skin must have been a disguise to keep her from looking exactly like her clones, but it had been knocked loose by the falling boxes. I rushed over and checked her pulse. It was strong. I turned to Judge. "Help me get her out of here."

But Judge didn't move. Her small frame seemed filled with tension, like a coiled spring waiting to explode.

Charlotte noticed it, too. "Judge? What is it? Why are you here?"

"Shhh," she whispered. Her eyes were darting around, looking into the shadows and dark corners. "Asyla is on this level."

My heart skipped a beat. "What?"

"I'm sorry," Judge said. "She broke away from me and headed here. I couldn't stop her. Turns out she is much stronger than either of us thought."

124

Before this news could sink in, there was a sound like a battle cry. Asyla soared through the air above our heads and slammed into ESCAPE BY A HAIR at full force.

ASYLA SMASHED INTO THE STATUE!

"No!" I shouted, unable to stop myself. For a moment, I forgot about the danger to us and thought only about the statue. After all, I had been hired to protect it.

Upon impact, the statue cracked in two, the halves falling away and smashing to the floor. Pieces of marble skittered in every direction. A tin box about the size of a bar of soap clattered to the floor. It must have been hidden inside the statue.

Asyla spun in midair and landed in a crouched position. She gazed up at us like a cat with the good fortune of finding three mice stuck on a glue trap.

"Hello," she purred. Then, still crouching, she plucked up the tin box.

We just stared at her.

"Is it Justine Pinkerton and her little friends to the rescue again?" she asked. "Is that the way history will remember this encounter?" Then to answer her own question, she added, "Not this time."

ASYLA PICKED AT THE LOCK.

I didn't say anything. Sometimes a detective just has to listen to get answers.

Asyla's fingers were working at the tiny lock on the tin box. "Aren't locks amazing inventions? No matter how advanced they get, you still need a key in order to open them."

"What are you talking about?" Charlotte said.

"Why, the key to this whole situation, of course." Asyla turned her eyes on Judge and me. "In this case, it would be an anagram. You people and your anagrams. Always so clever at solving them. Feverishly switching letters about here and there, and always cracking the case at just the last second."

There was a small click from the lock, but it still didn't open.

Asyla continued, "You have no idea how I laughed every time we met, and all of you would say my name: Notabe, Notabe, Notabe.

I mean really! Notabe's not even an anagram."

NOTABE...

I gazed at Asyla in shock. The image of her standing in the ruins of the statue of Mary Todd Lincoln and John Wilkes Booth seemed suddenly charged.

I could almost feel the pieces of the puzzle clicking into place in my brain. The answer must have been in the journals all along. For a moment, I was too surprised to speak. Asyla just grinned at me, clearly enjoying herself.

"NOT ABE," Judge and I said at the same time.

"EUREKA!" Asyla shouted, her voice echoing around the room. "Not Abe, indeed. As in 'not Abraham Lincoln.' And to think it only took you 125 years to figure it out!"

"I don't get it," Charlotte said.

Asyla made a face. "Then let me be the one to explain it to you, my dear. My great uncle was John Wilkes Booth. My mother changed our name from Booth to Notabe, and we made it our life's mission to make the lives of the Pinkertons miserable. They kept my mother from what's in this box so many years ago. Them and their good friends, the Fitzmorgans and Moories. The moment I heard the title of this statue, I knew why my clone wanted it It's something I tried desperately to get my hands on during my life." As if thinking out loud, she added, "All those years I spent developing cloning technology...and now, I don't really need it."

"What are you talking about?" Charlotte said.

"For being a copy of me, you really aren't very bright, are you?" Asyla said. "That night at the theater, Mrs. Lincoln nearly caught my great uncle. You might say she missed him by a hair."

With that, she gave one more twist and the tin box finally popped open. As Asyla gazed inside, her face filled with awe. "Look at that!" she breathed. "Isn't it beautiful?" She turned the box slightly toward us, and I could make out a small lock of...

"Hair!" I said.

"And now you must know why I wanted this statue so badly."

Judge breathed, "That hair..."

"Yes?" Asyla asked in a teasing tone. It was like dealing with someone who had her finger on the trigger of a gun. And that gun was pointed at us.

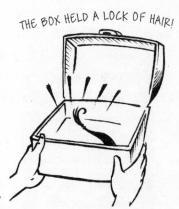

THE BOX HELD A LOCK OF HAIR!

I said, "That hair belongs to—"

"Ah! Only now you understand," she said triumphantly. "Only now when your time is up!" Her hand moved toward the lock of hair.

Judge and I dove forward at the same time to stop her. But we were too late. Asyla laid her hand on the hair.

There was a sharp hiss like the last bit of fuse burning down on a stick of dynamite.

I reached out toward her—

And there was a bright, violent explosion as the nanobots that made up Asyla flew apart. It threw Judge and me backward off our feet. We tumbled into Charlotte, and the three of us fell into a heap. As I tried to catch my breath, I felt something near my chest clicking and clacking.

Before us, the disorganized nano-material swirled violently. And using the DNA in the hair, it reorganized into the shape of a man.

Wearing a three-piece suit in the style of the 1860s, he looked to be about twenty-six. He had a head of curly brown hair above an oddly pale but handsome face. His eyes were the most distinctive thing about him. They burned like hot coals.

It was a man any historian would easily recognize.

The assassin John Wilkes Booth was standing before us. He ran his hands over his face and made his way over to the window, in the airlock door, where he could see his reflection. He touched his hair.

"My niece was right," he murmured. "She said hair samples were like seeds that could be used to 'grow' people. She knew it would take decades for science to catch up to the idea...but it did. And she brought me back." Then he noticed us watching him in the reflection. "Who are you?" he asked.

"We're the ones who brought you back," Judge lied, stalling for time.

Booth smiled for a moment and then cocked his head to the side as if he were accessing some internal memory. "No, I don't think so. My grand niece, Asyla, is still part of me. And like a wonderful director in

INFAMOUS ESCAPES!

John Wilkes Booth

After shooting President Abraham Lincoln on April 14, 1865, John Wilkes Booth leaped out of the Presidential Box at Ford's Theater in Washington, D.C. As the famous actor crashed onto the stage, he broke his left leg. Booth paused to deliver his last line onstage: "Sic semper tyrannis" ("Thus always with tyrants"), then ran, limping, out of the theater and escaped on horseback.

On April 26, Booth was trapped in a shed on a Virginia farm but refused to surrender even after it was set on fire. Booth was shot in the neck and dragged outside. Before dying, the clearly misguided villain whispered: "Tell my mother I did it for my country...."

my profession, that part of me is telling me exactly what needs to be done. It's time for the curtain to come down."

He took a step toward us. The dark gleam in his eyes made his violent intentions clear. Next to me, I felt Charlotte take a defensive stance, and I braced myself.

Suddenly, Teddy burst out of my jacket on the attack. He must have clicked on during my fall. Now he flicked himself off my body with his tiny back legs and launched himself at Booth. His loud, sharp barking pierced the air.

TEDDY LEAPED AT BOOTH!

He was trying to save us—

But Booth didn't even flinch. He just lashed out with one foot and kicked Teddy across the room. He bounced off a crate and slammed against the wall with a sickening crack. His bio-real eyes sparked and went dark as he slid to the floor.

I didn't cry out. That would just waste the opportunity that Teddy had given us. Instead, as if we were all of the same mind, Charlotte, Judge, and I rolled to Booth's right. We ducked behind a pile of crates, and crab-walked across the floor until we were hidden behind a wall of giant industrial barrels.

We were all breathing heavily but trying to keep it quiet. "Now what do we do?" Charlotte whispered. "Bring back Al Capone? How about Dracula?"

I didn't laugh at her joke, but she had a point. We had just helped to bring back one of the most notorious criminals of all time.

I listened carefully to make sure Booth wasn't nearby. I could hear him moving around on the other side of the level.

129

"If we can stall him long enough," I murmured to Judge, "he might go to sleep like you and Asyla did."

Judge shook her head. "If that were the case, he would have gone to sleep by now. I think the direct DNA source has changed things. I don't think he's going to have to stop to reboot."

"In that case," I said, "I need to get to my probe."

"Why?" Charlotte asked.

"Two days ago, before the nano-material went from Judge to Asyla, I forced it to travel through an apple. As they passed through, the nanobots picked up bacteria. The bacteria are a food source for the nanobots. All we need is a heat source to trigger a reaction. I can use my probe to make that heat."

I was surprised when they didn't question what I planned to do. I guessed desperate times called for desperate measures.

"Okay," Judge said. "Charlotte and I will keep Booth occupied while you get the probe."

They rushed back toward the airlock. "Judge!" I heard Charlotte call out to draw Booth's attention away from me. And it worked. From around the edge of a barrel, I saw him dart after them.

130

CARING FOR YOUR NEW NANOBOT

Follow these simple steps, and you'll be off to a good start:

1) First, find your 'bot. This is easier said than done. Most nanobots are less than 100 nanometers long. And a nanometer is one billionth of a meter—or the length of about 10 atoms placed end to end.

2) Learn what your 'bot is programmed to do. Some nanobots work alone, like those that act as surgeons in the capillaries of the human body. But many nanobots are made to work with others to form shapes that can work with humans. So your 'bot's factory programming might have to be changed if you want it to follow your commands.

3) Feed your 'bot right. It doesn't need much, but if you expect it to multiply and repair itself, then you have to give it a source of power. This could simply be electricity—or if you have a newer model, food.

I ran over to the broken boxes that covered Ms. Jenkins and quickly began searching for SHARP TEETH. I had just spotted the putrid green teeth when a hand wrapped around my ankle.

"Ah!" I shouted. The hand belonged to Ms. Jenkins, and she was looking up at me with dazed hatred. Her grasp was weak, and I jerked my leg free. Her eyes closed as she fell back into unconsciousness.

I reached carefully for SHARP TEETH and yanked it out of the debris.

The sound of Charlotte's screams filled the level.

I plucked my probe out of SHARP TEETH and shouted, "I'm coming!"

"Otis!" she cried from somewhere nearby.

I ran toward the sound. When I reached her, I could see why she'd been screaming. Booth had Judge in a headlock. She squirmed and kicked, but she was no match for him. He seemed to be squeezing the life out of her.

"Let her go!" I shouted.

"All right," he said. To my surprise, he tossed Judge aside. She tumbled in a heap next to the airlock. Charlotte rushed to her side. Booth cracked his knuckles as he eyed me hungrily. "I want to savor every last second of this experience, anyway."

131

Even then I thought, Am I really facing off against the man who killed Abraham Lincoln?

"Stand back," I told him and pointed the probe at him.

"And what do you have there?" Booth asked in a mocking tone as he took a step toward me.

I didn't want to be like the guy in virtual movies who talks too long and gives the bad guy a chance to attack. Without hesitating another moment, I pointed my probe at John Wilkes Booth and pressed the ON button.

Nothing happened.

"Ooooh, that was very frightening," Booth said sarcastically. "Is that the best you can do?"

"Just wait," I said, still holding out the probe. "It gets better. Much better."

BLAM!

There was a flash of light.

The probe had taken a second to heat up, but now the nanobots were overriding their programming in a feeding frenzy. They were disconnecting from each other as they desperately sought out a meal of bacteria.

It was as if someone had pressed a rewind button on Booth. His body began to shrink and his face to disintegrate. In his place, Asyla appeared once more.

But the disintegration didn't stop there. Suddenly, we were looking at a much younger Asyla...maybe six years old.

Then that Asyla was gone as well. In a long arc of streaming material, the nanobots flew across the room and straight into Judge's chest. She jerked slightly, and her body literally left the floor. She spun slowly as the whirlwind surrounded her.

THE SWARMING NANOBOTS PLOWED INTO JUDGE'S CHEST.

Judge aged before our eyes. As she grew taller, her hair and clothes changed, and I could see decades ticking by. Finally, the nanobots' food source ran out and they stopped swirling. When Judge came to rest, she looked to be about thirty years old.

She was gazing down at herself, so I couldn't see her expression. Was she okay?

133

"Judge...?"

She lifted her head. Her face broke out in a smile.

"You did it, Otis," Judge said, her voice more mature again. "Bully for you!" She stepped forward and gave me a hug.

I pulled back slightly and gestured to Charlotte. She joined us in the circle. "We did it together," I said.

"And just in time," Charlotte said. Over her shoulder, I could see what she meant. Through the thick glass of the small windows in the airlock doors, I could see that it was no longer black outside. Instead, it was cool blue with a yellow tinge.

We had just entered Earth's atmosphere.

THE ADULTS HAD ALL REGAINED CONSCIOUSNESS!

The first thing I did was find Teddy.

He had clicked off when his body struck the wall. But when I turned him back on, he started whirling and clacking furiously, as if he were still going after Booth. I assured him everything was okay, and he looked up at me with those soft bio-real eyes and blinked twice. "Good boy." I told him, and even Charlotte said, "That's one brave toy." I tucked Teddy safely back in my jacket pocket.

We made sure that Ms. Jenkins was securely but comfortably tied up. After putting helmets and gloves back on, we made our way carefully down the ladder to Level 1 then rushed up to the Common Room.

The room was bustling. Well, quietly bustling. Most of the adults were there, talking softly to one another. They all looked groggy and a little beaten up, but it was so wonderful to see them awake. Ms. Jenkins had been telling the truth. Apparently, the virus had an auto-destruct element. It had just kicked in a little earlier than she had planned.

Crockett looked up at us from where he was checking on Mrs. Benato, who sat on a loveseat with Lysa. He gave us the thumbs-up sign.

Mr. Bennett was sprawled on a couch, his head in his hands. I thought about telling him how SHARP TEETH had helped subdue Ms. Jenkins but decided it could wait.

I quickly scanned the room again. I saw Yves sitting with his parents. He gave me a small wave and a sheepish smile. I returned the smile, but my eyes kept moving. There! My mom and dad were sitting on a couch. As Charlotte rushed to her father, I sprinted

135

over to my parents. They
held out their arms to me and
the three of us shared a long,
long hug.

Feeling tears on my cheeks,
I pulled back just so I could
look at them.

"Crockett told us a little
about what's happened...," Dad
said, and then trailed off as he
looked over my shoulder.

I WAS SO GLAD MOM AND DAD WERE OKAY!

I saw he was gazing in wonder at Judge.

"Hello," Judge said, smiling. "I'm so glad you're feeling better.
You had us worried, you know."

"Oh, my," Mom said. "I think I'm sicker than I thought."

"No, it's okay, Mom. I'd like to introduce you to Judge Pinkerton."

Both of my parents knew Judge the way I had before this
Elevator trip: from the journals of our ancestors. She had been
woven into the fabric of our family.

My mom's eyes filled with tears. "How...?"

"Oh," Dad said in a husky voice, "I wish my mother were here
to see you."

Judge beamed at them both. "We've got a lot of catching up
to do."

I left them alone. As I was helping Crockett make the other
adults comfortable and get them something to eat, I kept an eye
on my parents and Judge.

I had spent my life uncovering fakes. So I felt like I knew a
real person. And that's what I saw when I looked at Judge—who was

composed of trillions of nanobots—a real person. But I knew not everyone would see her like that. There would be people, like Lysa, who were scared because they didn't know any better. And then there would be more dangerous people. The ones who might want to destroy Judge or keep her locked up because she was different.

About twenty minutes later, Judge joined me by the observation window. In silence, we watched Earth as it grew closer and closer.

I guess Judge was thinking along the same lines I'd been. She said, "I know from your hard drive and from what your parents just told me that I might not have any rights on Earth because I'm an artificial life form."

I wanted to tell her that wasn't true. But it was. Who knew what would happen to Judge when she got back to Earth? I looked at her. "Our laws need to catch up with technology."

"But that could be some time, couldn't it?" she asked.

I nodded. "Honestly, it could be years. When we reach Earth and they open those doors, I'm not sure what will happen to you."

Judge was quiet again for a moment. Then she said, "I wish there was some way for me to slip away when we reach Earth."

"That's going to be impossible," I told her, trying to be as truthful as possible. "We'll be met by Customs. There will be no way to sneak off without anyone knowing it. And once they have you in custody..."

You might never be free, I finished to myself.

"Could you change shape?" Charlotte asked from behind us. "Sorry to interrupt,

but maybe we could program you into..." Her voice trailed off. "But then you'd just be hiding who you really are."

Judge nodded. "And that's no way to live."

More silence. Finally, I said, "I have an idea. Come with me."

Charlotte and Judge followed me to Level 2. When we reached our destination, Charlotte seemed doubtful, but Judge clapped her hands together.

"Oh, yes!" she cried. "This is just perfect."

We were gazing up at the retrofitted biplane.

"It uses hover technology," I explained. "But the controls are the same as they would be on a regular biplane."

"A young man taught me to fly one of these old planes over a hundred years ago."

"I know," I said. "John Hatherford was the pilot's name."

Judge looked surprised for a moment. Then she smiled. "You read G. Codd's journal, so you know flying this won't be a problem for me."

"Are you sure about this?" Charlotte said, eyeing the plane.

138

"Absolutely," Judge answered without hesitation. "I need my freedom. I'll make my way in the world and wait for it to catch up."

I touched her arm. When Judge turned to look at me, I said, "But keep in touch."

"Always," Judge promised. We hugged. "Thank you," she whispered to me.

She embraced Charlotte and climbed into the open cockpit of the plane.

"We need to get inside the airlock," I said to Charlotte. "I can open the large cargo door from there. We're still pretty high up, so once the door's open, the air will be too thin and too cold for us."

Charlotte nodded. We opened the inner door of the airlock, stepped inside, and closed the door behind us. Through the small window, we could see the plane and Judge.

"Is she going to be okay?" Charlotte asked as I pressed my thumb on the keypad and gained access to the cargo door controls.

"Don't worry," I said. "The Climber is descending at a stable rate. And the hovercraft equipment on the biplane includes a powerful nuclear engine. Judge simply has to lift off and move the plane forward and she'll be free."

THUNK! THUNK!

I could practically feel the bolts sliding back as the cargo door unlocked. And then it slowly opened up and outward, like a flap lifting up from the side of the Elevator.

Judge rolled the plane to the edge. Then it lifted up and glided off the Elevator.

"Wow," Charlotte whispered next to me. "She's—"

"Incredible." I finished for her. I knew in my heart I would see Judge again someday.

139

Judge hovered for a moment, giving me one last thumbs-up and a grin. She mouthed, "See you soon!"

We watched her until the biplane was just a speck in the bright blue sky.

And then she was gone.

About two hours later, Charlotte and I waited in front of the main doors of the Climber. Our parents were standing in front of us. My mom and dad were telling a story to Mr. Noonan, who was laughing along.

We had reached the bottom of the ribbon about twenty minutes earlier. We now sat on the Elevator platform on Salmona Isle, a small rocky island in the middle of the Pacific Ocean.

The Elevator had come to rest with a loud hiss, as if the mechanical clamps were as tired as we were. The crews outside had been spraying down the outside with high-powered disinfectant, just in case we had brought back any extraterrestrials without realizing it.

"How will you explain that missing plane?" Charlotte asked me.

"I don't know," I said. And then couldn't resist grinning. "I guess I'll buy the owner a new one."

"And, how exactly will you do that?" She nudged me in the ribs.

"I plan on collecting a nice chunk of change."

Understanding lit her face. She smiled. "You're going to collect the reward money for recovering the statue?"

"You got it," I answered. "All the artwork on board has an automatic reward policy."

"Even though the statue is smashed into pieces?"

"Since it has been 'damaged,' the reward will be half," I explained. "But it's still a fortune. There will be plenty to buy a new plane."

"What will you do with the rest of the money?" she asked.

140

"I plan on making it my life's mission to ensure that private detectives are allowed to practice again."

I looked over at Mrs. Benato and Lysa. Crockett was standing with them, and Lysa was listening intently as he told her a story.

I realized Judge wasn't the only one who had a second chance to build a life. Asyla Notabe would live on in Mrs. Benato, Ms. Jenkins, Lysa...and in Charlotte.

She must have noticed my gaze on her. "What?" she asked a little self-consciously.

"I was just thinking about the future."

"And what do you see?"

I smiled. "I'd rather show you," I said.

A worker opened the door to the Climber from the outside, and cried, "Welcome home!"

Following in the footsteps of our parents, Charlotte and I walked out into the bright sunlight and onto planet Earth.

A NOTE FROM THE AUTHOR

This note is different than many others I've written for the Crime Through Time series. Normally, I'd tell you not to use this book to study for a history test. But unless you're reading this in 2032 or after, that's not going to be a problem. Just remember, Judge and the other characters are inventions of my imagination.

Most of the technology, however—such as cool uses for nanobots—is based on real scientific advances and might be right around the corner.

NASA is considering building a space elevator. There'd be no need for dangerous and expensive launches from Earth. Satellites and spacecraft could be sent off into space from the top of the elevator. Imagine: You might ride the space elevator someday.

Even with all this amazing technology in the story, I wanted Otis and his friends to rely on good, old-fashioned detective work to crack the case. Clever gadgets are no substitute for using your head in tricky situations.

Finally, one thing I loved about writing this book was letting Asyla show all her cards. Her character was like a seed I planted in the first book—and she finally got to blossom here. Even though she's the villain, it felt great to finally unleash her!

Like Otis, I have the feeling we may not have seen the last of Asyla . . . or Judge!

Yours in time,

Bill Doyle

ABOUT THE AUTHOR

Bill Doyle was born in Lansing, Michigan, and wrote his first mystery when he was eight. He loved seeing the shock on people's faces when they discovered the identity of the story's villain—and knew then that he was hooked on writing. Bill has written for Sesame Workshop, LeapFrog, Scholastic, ROLLING STONE, TIME FOR KIDS, and the Museum of Natural History. He lives in New York City with a mysterious dachshund named Esme.

HOW ?.
WILL THE...
ESC...?

FIND THE
CODE!
OR IS IT
TOO
LA...

3
SAME
FAMILY
WORLD'S

Check out these other gripping
Crime Through Time™ books!
Now in stores!

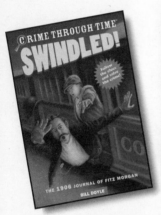

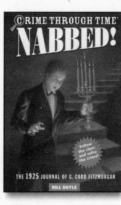

EXTRA! EXTRA!
Don't forget to read the newspaper in the back of each book!